CW00402118

Critical Guides to French Texts

80 Genet: Les Nègres

Critical Guides to French Texts

EDITED BY ROGER LITTLE, WOLFGANG VAN EMDEN,
DAVID WILLIAMS

GENET

Les Nègres

J.P.Little

Lecturer in French
St Patrick's College, Drumcondra

Grant & Cutler Ltd
1990

ISBN 0 7293 0323 3

I.S.B.N. 84-599-3063-7

DEPÓSITO LEGAL: V. 1.388 - 1990

Printed in Spain by
Artes Gráficas Soler, S.A., Valencia
for
GRANT & CUTLER LTD
55-57 GREAT MARLBOROUGH STREET, LONDON, W1V 2AY

Contents

For Dominic and Rebecca

Prefatory Note

For ease of access the edition´ used is the paperback published in Gallimard's 'Collection Folio', no.1180. In the bibliography at the end of the present study, this volume figures as no.10, and is referred to throughout the text according to the style '(*10*, p.36)'. Other bibliographical references follow the same pattern.

Precise acknowledgements on points of detail are given in the notes to the text. In addition, however, my grateful thanks go to the following: to the Camargo Foundation, Cassis, for an unequalled site and facilities in which to pursue my reflections; to St Patrick's College, Drumcondra, Dublin, for leave of absence enabling me to concentrate on the project; to the library of St Patrick's College and to the Service d'Inter-Prêt of the Bibliothèque Municipale de Marseille for assistance in obtaining material; to my former students in Fourah Bay College, Freetown, Sierra Leone, and at St Patrick's College, for the way in which they enlarged my understanding of the difficulties of the text, and illuminated it by their perceptions; and finally to my husband, for his support and scrupulousness of attention at all stages of this project.

J.P.L.
Cassis, France

Introduction

'Réfléchissez un moment sur ce qu'on
appelle au théâtre "être vrai". Est-ce y
montrer les choses comme elles sont
en nature? Aucunement. Le vrai en
ce sens ne serait que le commun.'
(Diderot, *Paradoxe sur le comédien*)

Les Nègres opens with a challenge. In the course of his introductory
speech, Archibald, the master of ceremonies, states the Blacks'
objective: so that the white audience will not be disturbed by the
nature of the 'drame qui déjà se déroule ici', the aim of the spectacle
will be to 'rendre la communication impossible'. In this way Genet
from the outset defies traditional theatrical norms, where
communication is seen as an essential part of the dramatic
experience.

There is thus at work in this play a radical questioning of the
nature of the theatre itself. One of the most fascinating aspects of *Les
Nègres*, and one which I intend to pursue throughout this study, is
the way in which the play brings us up sharply against questions
such as 'what is a theatre? what is an actor, a spectator? what
relationship is there between them?' (cf.*40*, p.4). In this, of course,
Genet is in the mainstream of avant-garde theatre in the twentieth
century. But the form which his questioning takes is frequently
unlike anything used by other experimental dramatists of the age.
'Experimental' theatre is concerned with producing new 'rules' for
dramatic performances, because the dramatist has something to say
which cannot be said according to the old rules. But Genet is not

interested in constructing new formulae. He does in fact accept certain traditional principles of dramatic creation: for him theatre is an event which happens on stage, in front of an audience, it uses actors clearly identified as such, who perform to a pre-established text. Genet accepts these conventions then — but only to flout them by turning them upside down, by creating fissures in what was reassuringly solid, to reveal a gaping lack of substance underneath. As Bernard Dort so aptly puts it in a comment on Genet's attitude to theatre, 'Genet ne le célèbre que pour mieux le détruire' (*34, p.*128). He is thus 'experimental' in the sense of radically subversive.

To illustrate this, let us take a commonplace of the avant-garde, the way in which in the twentieth century, and especially since the formulations of Artaud, the theatre has moved away from the idea of the play as a written text to which was added a certain staging, décor, costumes etc., in order to 'realise' it in performance. Genet, with the avant-garde in general, is deeply conscious rather of what is now referred to as the 'performance text' as a complex of messages which go beyond the merely verbal, exploiting not only speech but gesture and a whole range of phenomena that operate in space rather than time. In the celebrated preface to *Les Bonnes*, he expresses his distaste for the coarseness and exhibitionism of traditional Western theatre, preferring rather 'un art qui serait un enchevêtrement profond de symboles actifs, capables de parler au public un langage où rien ne serait dit mais tout pressenti' (*11*, p.12). Ideally, he would wish the traditional notion of 'character', with its emphasis on psychological realism, to disappear, giving place to '[des] signes aussi éloignés que possible de ce qu'ils doivent d'abord signifier', so that 'ces personnages ne fussent plus sur la scène que la métaphore de ce qu'ils devaient représenter' (*11*, p.13). Clearly, Genet is here going beyond a predominantly language-orientated theatre and, inspired by oriental models, is seeking a more universal sign-system.

What happens in practice, however, is that the sign-system which he evolves, using all the physical and symbolic potential of the stage as a location in space, is used not to communicate with the audience in a positive way, but to confuse and disturb, to rouse the spectators from their comfortable world of one-to-one relationships where the 'meaning' of signs and symbols is immediately clear, and plunge them into a threatening void where meaning is expected but none, apparently, forthcoming. Take for instance the opening tableau of *Les Nègres*: before a word is spoken, the audience receives a visual impression of a group of blacks formally attired in evening-dress — but wearing yellow shoes. What is one to make of the shoes? The conventional dress conveys one message, the footwear flouts it and conveys a completely different one. Not only does there seem to be no apparent reason for these contradictory signs when they first appear, but they are given no rational explanation in the course of the play either. They disturb, because we are used to 'reading' the information we have in front of us; we need the signs we encounter to 'make sense'. In Roger Blin's highly-acclaimed first production of *Les Nègres* in October 1959 (which Genet said was 'de l'ordre de la perfection' [*10*, p.97]), it appears he used an arbitrary change of pitch and pace in order to disturb the audience (*40*, p.147), who thus had no opportunity to sink reassured into the familiar. The literal reality of a stage sign is built up by Genet to a certain point, only to be undercut by a disturbing counter-sign, just as the clients in the brothel portrayed in *Le Balcon* 'veulent tous que tout soit le plus vrai possible... Moins quelque chose d'indéfinissable, qui fera que ce n'est pas vrai' (*1*, p.73). On stage, this deliberate introduction of a principle of non-coherence and contradiction both destroys the illusion (in the sense of an imitation of reality) so that the spectator no longer believes in the reality of what he is being shown, and establishes it, by underlining that it is only 'play-acting'. Genet is acutely aware of the special status of theatrical representation, where an ordinary object such as a chair, for instance, both partakes and does not partake of the everyday reality accorded to it: it is 'real' in that it is a solid, physical object used by real actors on a real stage, but the audience cannot have with it the relationship they could have with a 'real' chair: it has no part in their everyday lives, they cannot sit on it, move it around, etc. (cf.*43*, p.46). Throughout *Les Nègres*, Genet explores this frontier between the real and the not-real,

perverting the interpretation of meaning, adding a question-mark to
the notion of meaning itself.

In spite of Genet's refusal to make unambiguous statements
regarding what we have on the stage in front of us, we are, of course,
nonetheless inevitably drawn to questions of meaning. In a play
which so superbly underlines the nature of theatre itself (Dort calls it
'non seulement théâtre *dans* le théâtre, mais encore théâtre *sur* le
théâtre' (*34*, p.128), where illusion and reality seem so inextricably
mingled, can one not tease out at least something of what Genet is
trying to say? Is any attempt to get below the sparkling surface to the
depths beneath doomed to failure? The question already presupposes
a level of appearance beyond which one can probe, which is perhaps
totally inappropriate. What can then be said of this play, what lines
of questioning can viably be pursued in the course of a study such as
this?

If one asks the question 'What is this play "about"?', then
clearly one is immediately thrown back on the notion that it is a play
'about' theatre, theatre with all its articulations revealed. 'Nous nous
embellissons pour vous plaire', says Archibald (*10*, p.28). 'Ce soir
nous jouerons pour vous' (ibid.). Genet's use of theatrical sub-codes,
of all the apparatus that tells an audience it is in the theatre, is one of
considerable interest and originality, and will be pursued throughout
this study. *Les Nègres* is also, equally obviously, 'about' blacks in
some sense or other. Chapter One will concern itself with Genet's
interpretation of the black world, and the way in which he uses this
world as an objective correlative for another, more private world.
These two aspects, the theatre and the portrayal of the black world,
represent a thematic approach which will, I believe, yield useful
insights into what Genet is doing with theatre in this play. It is
possible also, however, on a more literal level, to analyse *Les Nègres*
in a linear way, in terms of the events which happen — or appear to
happen — in the course of the play.

There are three main linear movements — this for want of a
better word: one can hardly call them 'plots', so far removed are they
in their inconclusiveness from what would normally be termed 'plot'.
Each is distinguished not only by its subject-matter, but also by its

mode of representation, from the ritualistic to the semi-naturalistic, which accounts for much of the variety of tone in the play.

The central movement concerns the ritual re-enactment of the rape and murder by the blacks of a white woman whose corpse is apparently in the coffin which lies centre-stage throughout most of the play. This act of revenge for the humiliations meted out to the blacks by the white world is countered by the revenge set in motion by the members of the 'white' Court, who act as spectators to the ceremony, for the murder of the white woman. This revenge is not achieved, however, since after a confrontation between black and white, the white Court is massacred by the blacks. The ritual nature of the whole sequence is emphasised by the fact that at the end all is in place for its re-enactment 'jusqu'à la mort de la race' (*10*, p.87).

The second linear movement runs parallel to the first, but remains to the end much more obscure. The audience becomes aware of it visually from the beginning, in the person of Ville de Saint-Nazaire, since he, unlike the blacks in evening dress and the Court in their costumes symbolising white power, is clad in ordinary day clothes and goes barefoot. His language too is everyday, and never attains the ritual, poetic intensity of the blacks performing the ceremony. (His name, incidentally, is that of a ship that plied the infamous triangle of the slave-trade.) Through his comings and goings in the course of the play we gradually become aware of a drama which has been conducted off-stage, where a traitor to the black cause has apparently been judged and executed. We are told at the end that this is the 'real' action, whereas what the audience was witnessing on stage was a mere cover-up. There is a clear parallel here with the action in *Le Balcon*, where Genet sustains the same counterpoint between the ritual action seen on stage, and the revolution which we are told is going on outside.

The third strand concerns the love-affair between two of the central characters, the 'murderer' Village, and the ironically-named prostitute Vertu. They distinguish themselves from the hate-ritual precisely through their love for each other which, we are led to believe, concerns their life 'off-stage' and is therefore not given as part of theatrical reality, except in so far as it makes them reluctant to play their parts in the ritual. The question of the extent to which one can talk of their 'off-stage' lives is one that will be confronted at a later point in this study, as will that of the reality or otherwise of off-stage events in the context of the Ville de Saint-Nazaire episode.

To reduce the events of the play to something which can be presented discursively is already, however, a certain travesty. Throughout any discussion of 'what happens', we must retain firmly the notion that things are not what they seem. Or even that things are not: what they seem is all. Everything both is and is not what it is represented to be. There is a profound ambiguity for example in the attitude to the audience evoked at the beginning of this introduction. Hatred is both the means and end to the deliberate breaking of communication between the on-stage actors and the audience: and yet this hatred would not exist without its opposite, love. Indeed, hatred is a kind of measure of love: as Genet says in his autobiographical *Journal du voleur*, 'A la gravité des moyens que j'exige pour vous écarter de moi, mesurez la tendresse que je vous porte' (*7*, p.235). Village expresses the same conflict when he attempts to express his feelings for Vertu: 'Je vous hais de remplir de douceur mes yeux noirs. Je vous hais de m'obliger à ce dur travail qui consiste à vous écarter de moi, à vous haïr' (*10*, p.46). Treason — another theme to which we shall return — was considered by Genet to be the supreme crime, because it demanded the supreme sacrifice. The traitor has to know how to 'briser les liens d'amour qui l'unissaient aux hommes' (*7*, p.276). In this way the act of treason becomes beautiful: 'Indispensable pour obtenir la beauté: l'amour. Et la cruauté la brisant' (ibid.).

It is a strangely inverted world, therefore, that Genet presents to us in *Les Nègres*, a world in which everything reflects its opposite and meaning is deliberately obscured. The reasons why this should be so and the means by which Genet translates his vision into theatre will form the central questions in the pages that follow.

1. A Black World

'Les mots noirs sur la page blanche
américaine sont quelquefois raturés,
effacés. Les plus beaux disparaissent
mais c'est ceux-là — les disparus —
qui forment le poème — ou plutôt le
poème du poème.'
(Genet, *Un Captif amoureux*)

The immediate stimulus to the writing of *Les Nègres* came in 1955
from the actor Raymond Rouleau, who asked Genet to write a play
for black actors. He in fact gave up the idea of staging it, because of
the difficulty of finding sufficient black actors in Paris, but the idea
was taken up at the beginning of 1958 by Roger Blin, who was
working at the time with a recently-formed company of black actors,
Les Griots. This company, made up mainly of amateurs, with one or
two professionals, from all parts of the French-speaking world, had
come together in 1956 and taken part, with Sartre's *Huis clos*, in the
Concours régional de théâtre universitaire at Evreux, and had
subsequently taken the production to Africa. When Genet gave Blin
permission to work on *Les Nègres*, there followed nearly two years
of hard work during which the cast came to grips with the text and
Blin worked them gradually into a coherent whole, standardising
their varying French accents. The success of the play, when Blin
finally managed to stage it at the Théâtre de Lutèce in October 1959,
after a long and problem-ridden search for a theatre, owed a great
deal to Blin's staging, as Genet was the first to acknowledge.

In terms of source-material for Genet's play, one should
perhaps mention first, albeit in passing, the ethnographical film
made in 1955 by Jean Rouch, *Les Maîtres-fous*. Rouch records the
ritual performances of a West African tribe, who 'liberate'

themselves from the psychological burden of their colonial masters
by incorporating into their ceremonies masks representing colonial
officials (see *51*, p.211). Given the parallel with Genet's use of
masks in *Les Nègres*, it is tempting to see here a source, especially in
view of the date of the film's appearance, but Claude Sarraute
maintains that Genet had not seen Rouch's film when he wrote *Les
Nègres*.[1]

    A more certain source, certain because recorded by Genet
himself, has recently become available in the form of a short text
beginning 'L'art est le refuge...', and published in *Les Nègres au port
de la lune*, a collection of writings focusing on the production of *Les
Nègres* at the Centre Dramatique National Bordeaux Aquitaine (*13*).
In it Genet reveals the immediate inspiration for the play: 'Le point
de départ, le déclic, me fut donné par une boîte à musique où les
automates étaient quatre Nègres en livrée s'inclinant devant une
petite princesse de porcelaine blanche' (*13*, p.101). The visual image
immediately recalls the opening scene of *Les Nègres*, with the
Blacks in evening dress dancing a minuet around the — supposed —
white woman's corpse, especially since Genet notes that what he
calls 'ce charmant bibelot' dated from the eighteenth century, and the
opening of the play with its strains of *Don Giovanni* recalls precisely
that period. It is both an evocation and a macabre parody. What
fascinates Genet is the question: 'que se passe-t-il donc dans l'âme de
ces personnages obscurs que notre civilisation a acceptés dans son
imagerie, mais toujours sous l'apparence légèrement bouffone d'une
cariatide de guéridon, de porte-traîne ou de serveur de café
costumé?' (ibid). They, like the Blacks in the play, are insubstantial:
'ils sont en chiffon, ils n'ont pas d'âme' (ibid). What can be the
relationship between the white world and these figures? 'Quand nous
voyons les Nègres, voyons-nous autre chose que de précis et
sombres fantômes nés de notre désir?' (ibid). What are they thinking
of us? What game are they playing? What too is their relationship to
the French language, to what Genet calls 'ma langue, orgueil de ma

---

[1] Claude Sarraute, *Le Monde* (30 oct. 1959): 'Genet avait déjà publié sa
pièce quand il vit ce beau film documentaire retraçant des faits analogues à
ceux qu'il venait de porter à la scène'.

race et de mon peuple' (ibid)? He cannot imagine that, being essentially exterior to it, they do not hate it as they are obliged to learn it. What can the French language say about them that is true? 'Les figures qui vont surgir de cette langue peuvent-elles être autre chose que la projection là, sur la scène, de ces fantômes en quoi je voudrais métamorphoser de vrais Nègres?' (*13*, p.102).

This text gives a fascinating insight into the image that sparked off *Les Nègres*, an image that is full of theatricality and ceremony, but which immediately suggested to him the lack of substance that is at the heart of *Les Nègres*.

Another theatrical image which Genet himself proposes as a source for his play appears in an early version of *Le Balcon*: it seems that in this version he used the figure of a black man disguised as a white in order to humiliate a white woman made up as a black. The idea seemed so full of potential that he removed it from the text of *Le Balcon* in order to develop it into a complete play.[2] If this is so, then the idea has gained immeasurably by its development from what seems to have been portrayed as a private sexual fantasy to something of much broader and more universal significance.

There is ample evidence, however, of Genet's interest in the black world, and of his occasional use of black characters in his writings prior to the creation of *Les Nègres*. Boule-de-Neige, in his first play, *Haute surveillance*, springs to mind immediately, although he is used as a distant archetype aspired to by the prison inmates portrayed by Genet, and never actually seen on stage. His reputation in crime is recognised by everyone, from his cell-mates to convicts in every prison in France. According to Lefranc, a fellow-prisoner, 'Il brille, il rayonne. Il est noir et il éclaire les deux mille cellules. Personne ne pourra l'abattre. C'est lui le véritable chef de la forteresse... Boule de Neige, c'est un roi' (*5*, pp.184, 185). This character is perhaps drawn from Genet's own experience, since Magnan records that Genet at one time shared a cell with a certain

---

[2] I am indebted for this information to M. Jean-Bernard Moraly, of the Hebrew University of Jerusalem, to whom it was communicated by Genet himself in an interview.

Clément Village, a black prisoner whose name is clearly recalled by Genet in *Les Nègres* (*24*, p.59).

One must also recall the general atmosphere in Paris, where Genet was for a fair amount of time, in the forties and fifties. It was a time of consolidation for the great names of *négritude*, whose revolt against white supremacy in all its forms in the thirties was now crowned with political power, albeit within the French system. In the late forties, Senghor, Césaire and Damas were all successively elected *députés*, giving them a high profile in Paris. In 1947 the review *Présence Africaine* was born simultaneously in Paris and Dakar, with the support of such French intellectuals as Gide, Sartre, Mounier and Camus.[3] On the literary front, too, these years saw the publication of major works such as Jacques Roumain's *Bois d'ébène* in 1945, while Césaire's *Les Armes miraculeuses* appeared in 1946, and his *Soleil cou coupé* in 1948. In 1947 Damas brought black poets to the notice of the French public with his *Première anthologie des poètes d'outre-mer*, while Senghor's seminal *Anthologie de la nouvelle poésie nègre et malgache*, with its preface by Sartre, 'Orphée noir', was published in 1948. Indeed, many of Sartre's observations in 'Orphée noir' read like a commentary on *Les Nègres*. Genet's preoccupation with metaphorical, metaphysical death is echoed by Sartre's 'il s'agit ... pour le noir de mourir à la culture blanche pour renaître à l'âme noire' (*67*, p.xxiii). But at the same time, paradoxically, 'il s'agit ... de devenir ce qu'il est' (ibid). The difficulty and discipline of the path to be followed are indicated for the black world in general by Sartre's definition of the black's vocation to 'reconquérir son unité existentielle de nègre ... par une ascèse progressive' (ibid). Genet could not have failed to be aware of this general movement in the direction of black consciousness, especially given his close relationship with Sartre over the period.

In terms of his own personal perceptions, Genet has always been frank about the erotic appeal exercised on him by blacks and Arabs. In the interview he gave to Hubert Fichte, he wonders

---

[3] For a history of the period, see Lilyan Kesteloot, *Les Ecrivains noirs de langue française: naissance d'une littérature*, Brussels: Editions de l'Institut de Sociologie (Université Libre de Bruxelles), 1963.

whether his later commitment to the Black Panthers and the
Palestinian cause would have been possible without this attraction
(*16*, p.29). *Les Nègres* uses this erotic appeal, though it is notable
that, unlike the novels and the early plays, there is virtually no
homosexual element in his portrayal of the blacks. The Valet — in
any case disguised as a white — is the obvious exception to this rule,
but he is portrayed as a caricature, not intended to be taken seriously,
at least on this particular level.

In the same interview with Fichte, Genet admits to a certain
curiosity regarding the issue of race. Does the concept mean
anything? Are there inferior and superior races (*16*, p.32)? He puts
the question more fundamentally still in the preamble to the play,
when he tells how he was asked by an actor to write a play for
blacks: 'Mais, qu'est-ce que c'est donc un noir? Et d'abord, c'est de
quelle couleur?' (*10*, p.15). The significance of this question is not
necessarily obvious at once, and we will have cause to return to it
again in this chapter, but some immediate light can be shed on it
perhaps by turning to Sartre's 'Orphée noir', where he asks a similar
question, 'what is *négritude*?' Is it a state of fact, a condition into
which one is born, or something to which one aspires? 'Est-ce une
donnée de fait ou une valeur?... Est-ce une explication systématique
de l'âme noire ou un Archétype platonicien qu'on peut indéfiniment
approcher sans jamais y atteindre?' (*67*, pp.278-79). Similarly
Genet's blacks: they are *nègres* in the sense that this is what they are
condemned to be by the white world; this is their situation, one from
which there is no escape. But at the same time blackness is a state
which they spend their whole time trying to attain. 'Que les Nègres
se nègrent...', says Archibald (*10*, p.60), and the whole ceremony
revolves around this striving towards the goal of more complete
blackness. The ambiguity is the same: where they differ is in their
respective attitudes to the goal. *Négritude* as a state to be sought
after is always presented as something positive, the validation of
blackness in the face of a hostile or indifferent white world, whereas
Genet's blacks accept only reluctantly the role thrust upon them;
their defiance is made more desperate by the knowledge that they are
condemned to it, as a prisoner to his cell. In Archibald's words,

'Nous sommes sur cette scène semblables à des coupables qui, en prison, joueraient à être des coupables' (*10*, p.49).

This is so because in the end for Genet the black world is conditioned and, in a certain sense, totally created by its white counterpart. Black and white are presented in the play as completely interdependent. As Félicité says, 'Si vous êtes la lumière et que nous soyons l'ombre, tant qu'il y aura la nuit où vient sombrer le jour...' (she breaks off, as the Queen interrupts 'Je vais vous faire exterminer') then continues: 'Sotte, que vous seriez plate, sans cette ombre qui vous donne tant de relief' (*10*, pp.103-04). Interestingly, the black American writer James Baldwin makes use of the same idea of black-white interdependence in the following passage, which is worth quoting in full because of its relevance to Genet:

> Je n'étais pas un Noir, jusqu'à ce que l'Europe vienne me chercher dans mon village. J'avais la seule civilisation qu'un être humain puisse avoir: celle de mon village.
>
> La violence de ma rencontre avec l'Europe a fait de moi un Noir: c'est ce que l'Europe a dit. Mais la violence de cette rencontre a aussi fait de l'Européen un Blanc. C'est très dur d'être un Blanc! C'est, en fait, impossible, sans ce témoin absolument indispensable: cette créature contrainte à être un Noir selon les critères du Blanc.[4]

Baldwin feels himself to be a creation of Europe, just as Genet's blacks depend for their existence on the white world. Because, ultimately, to understand Genet's fascination for the blacks he portrays in his play, and the appropriateness of his choice of material, it is not sufficient to look only at the ethos of the times, or Genet's personal sexuality. It is necessary also to cast a glance at Genet's origins, and the singular nature of his childhood and youth.

To do this is not to ignore the formidable obstacles hampering any attempt to assess Genet's life. Whole areas of it have, at least until recently, remained obscure, and such details as Genet himself

---

[4] Entretien avec James Baldwin, propos recueillis par Hervé Prudon, *Le Nouvel Observateur* (25 avril 1983), p.64.

revealed, either in person or through Sartre's monumental study, *Saint-Genet, comédien et martyr,* have been seen more as seminal moments demanding interpretation than as a genuine attempt at chronology in the normal sense. Since Genet's death in 1986, however, there have been several attempts at radical reappraisal, among the most notable being Albert Dichy and Pascal Fouché's *Jean Genet, essai de chronologie 1910-1944 (23)* and Jean-Bernard Moraly's *Jean Genet, la vie écrite (26),* which continues the story up to the present. Setting out to establish the real facts of Genet's life, these works effectively demolish the myth of the unhappy childhood, of the literary *oeuvre* springing from nowhere: as Moraly says, 'dans le meilleur des cas, la mémoire de Genet est sélective. Du matériel vécu, Genet ne conserve que ce qui peut servir à l'image qu'il a bâtie de lui-même' *(26,* p.9).

To a large extent, however, the revelation that what had been accepted previously as fact is largely fiction only serves to underline Genet's need for self-dramatisation, his need not merely to make literature out of life but, having created his own image, to become totally identified with it. The Genet as constructed after the event is at least as revealing as the more pedestrian one that can be teased out of patient biographical research, however valuable the latter is. The poetic truth of the myth, after all, is the truth that is reflected in the novels and plays.

It is therefore in my view inevitable to take into account Sartre's study, in spite of its limitations regarding fact and its perspective as a piece of existentialist psychoanalysis. Critics have in any case always been divided over it: Richard Coe, for example, bases his excellent philosophically orientated study of Genet (see *22*) on Sartre's insights, while the anonymous commentator of *La Quinzaine littéraire,* presenting *Un Captif amoureux* and the articles of *Etudes palestiniennes,* considers that 'l'interprétation de Sartre ... est sans prise sur ce qui est le problème de Genet'.[5] But Genet himself seems to have taken it seriously: the 'legend' has it that he was so shattered by it that he did not write another word for six years. Moraly holds that Genet was by this time 'engagé dans un

---

[5] *La Quinzaine littéraire,* no. 471 (1 oct. 1986), p.4.

voyage esthétique vers le rien' (*26*, p.109) but accepts that it was the cause of a cooling of the relationship between Sartre and Genet. I have already noted the extent to which Sartrian language is reflected in *Les Nègres*, and many of the texts written during or after the period of his friendship with Sartre bear clear traces of Sartre's influence, including the semi-autobiographical *Journal du voleur*. Genet also claims that the *prise de conscience* provoked by Sartre's analysis provided the necessary passage from the early prison novels to the later work for the theatre (*15*, p.21).

Let us resume then briefly the essentials of what Sartre says, in so far as it is relevant to a study of *Les Nègres*. Sartre goes back to Genet's rejection by his parents at birth, and his placement with peasant foster-parents in the Morvan, where he spent an uneventful early childhood, with respect for people, property and religion, apparently accepting the values of rural society. At one point or another, however — Sartre is as vague about its actual timing as Genet habitually was — there occurred the event that was to turn into the central myth of Genet's existence: the child was caught stealing, and was thereby branded a thief. Genet had the misfortune of being fostered by people for whom property was everything: as a foster-child, he could inherit nothing, own nothing, and so was nothing. The obvious way therefore to acquire being and status was through theft. But, says Sartre, the moment Genet was accused of being a thief was the moment of death for the child Genet, and all his future career was destined to be marked by a negative sign. Rejected at birth, he is again rejected by the society he aspires to join, and this rejection creates in Genet a sense of void: 'Issu du néant, cet enfant n'a rien, n'est rien, son être a la substantialité du non-être' (*28*, p.28). He is branded by society around him as 'l'autre', 'le Mal', but being unable to identify with this image, he will lack henceforth any sense of being, and will spend his life in the vain pursuit of this 'Autre'. For, in a sense, Genet accepts the definition given him by society. Since things are thus, he must will them thus, and be what others wish him to be. He continues to steal, therefore, but the motivation has become inverted: 'Il volait parce qu'il "était" voleur; désormais c'est pour "être" voleur qu'il vole' (*28*, p.85). Genet himself confirms this in the *Journal du voleur*. He explains how he sank further and further into crime in the following terms: 'à chaque accusation portée contre moi, fût-elle injuste, du fond du cœur je répondrai oui. A peine avais-je prononcé ce mot ... en moi-même je sentais le besoin de devenir ce qu'on m'avait accusé d'être' (7, p.198).

The relevance of several of the themes suggested here by Sartre to an analysis of *Les Nègres* is not hard to establish. Like Genet himself, his blacks have a void at the centre of their being, and from this situation of void they aspire to be what they are not and cannot be. They exist as blacks only in the eyes of the whites, and have not chosen their identity, which has been given them by the superior power of their white masters. But, having received their identity from elsewhere, which necessitated the 'death' of their true identity, they decide to assume it totally. As Archibald says, 'Nous sommes ce qu'on veut que nous soyons, nous le serons donc jusqu'au bout absurdement' (*10*, p.122). Bernard Dort sees in this metamorphosis the moment of birth of Genet's theatre: 'Pour s'opposer au monde, Genet ne se revendique pas tel qu'il est; il se transforme d'abord en celui que les autres voient en lui' (*34*, p.130). He is thus always outside himself, always striving towards an alien image that can never be attained. The verb 'to be' escapes Genet, as it escapes his blacks. He can neither say 'I am' in the sense 'I exist', nor 'I am' with a complement such as 'a thief', since he is alienated from this as from other definitions. He exists in a state of permanent ontological crisis.

It is noteworthy for our purposes how much of this psychology is reproduced in the analyses of black writers such as Franz Fanon and Albert Memmi. For Memmi, one of the chief problems of the colonised is that '[il] n'arrive presque jamais à coïncider avec lui-même' (*66*, p.175). He accepts the definition of the coloniser, always expressed as a lack in the coloniser's eyes: 'il commence par s'accepter ... comme négativité' (*66*, p.173). The coloniser is always thus either the model or the antithesis. Graham Dunstan Martin, in his study of *Les Nègres*, shows how the play reflects colonialist attitudes, by invoking Jung's theory of 'the shadow'. The blacks on stage are then the projection of the white audience's 'shadow', that repressed complex of fears and attributes that it cannot cope with. In this sense, they are not real, and the ultimate driving force of the play is white racial attitudes (*53, passim*). The fears of the white Court, as well as the gap between reality and their understanding of it, can be seen in parodic form when the Queen asks fearfully 'Et... et... s'ils étaient réellement noirs? Et même, s'ils étaient vivants?' (*10*, pp.95-96).

Genet shows an instinctive understanding of this psychology. He in fact terms himself a black whose skin happens to be pink and white — but definitely a black (*16*, p.26). One of the black actors who played in the original Blin production, Robert Liensol, paid him the compliment of saying in an interview that 'il aurait pu être un noir lui-même'.[6] Genet's identification is complete firstly because of the history of oppression and dependence from which the black race suffered. Like Genet, they are natural outsiders, which explains why, in the novel *Querelle de Brest*, Querelle, after committing a murder, has the impression of being black, different from the white and non-criminal community around him.

It is possible to see now the sense of the second part of Genet's question at the beginning of the play: 'Qu'est-ce donc un noir? Et d'abord, c'est de quelle couleur?' Some blacks are black; others are pink, yellow, what you will, just as some blacks are white, as Diouf was metamorphosed at the end of *Les Nègres*. The blacks are white society's outcasts, the most completely outcast it is possible to be, since the condemnation is permanent unless, as in the case of Diouf, there is treason. The drama takes place on an ontological plane; blacks cannot change, as a thief could, in theory, become a reformed character. They can only become more fully black.

---

6 See Maria Craipeau, 'En répétition: *Les Nègres* de Jean Genet', *France-Observateur* (22 oct. 1959). It is interesting to compare Rimbaud's identification of himself with 'un nègre', with all its pejorative overtones: 'Oui, j'ai les yeux fermés à votre lumière. Je suis une bête, un nègre. Mais je puis être sauvé. Vous êtes de faux nègres, vous maniaques, féroces, avares. Marchand, tu es nègre; magistrat, tu es nègre; général, tu es nègre; empereur, vieille démangeaison, tu es nègre: tu as bu d'une liqueur non taxée, de la fabrique de Satan'. 'Une Saison en enfer', *Œuvres complètes*, Bibl. de la Pléiade, 1972, p.97.

This natural sympathy with black revolt explains why Genet was able to identify himself so readily with the Black Panther movement in America in the early seventies. In *Un Captif amoureux* he tells how with the Panthers he realised an old dream 'où des étrangers — mais au fond plus semblables à moi que mes compatriotes — m'ouvriraient à une vie nouvelle' (*2*, p.116). He clearly felt at one with them in their hatred of the white world and their desire to destroy it (*17*, p.38). Like him, they were motivated by pure negativity, 'travaillés par des forces "a" '(*2*, p.350). And, like Genet's blacks, who are concerned only to increase the rift between the black world and the white (*10*, p.26), 'les Panthères devaient s'ouvrir au monde par des brèches et des entailles, par du sang' (*2*, pp.350-51).

If this were the extent of Genet's commitment to these revolutionaries, it would no doubt seem a fairly banal siding with the underdog on the part of one who felt aggrieved at his rejection by society. But Genet goes much further, and gives a highly individual interpretation to their revolt which illuminates retrospectively his theatre in general, and *Les Nègres* in particular. What interests him in the Panthers, beyond their political stance, is the way in which they cultivate their image, although by doing so, in the eyes of some, they are in danger of becoming so absorbed in it that they are lost to revolutionary action. '[Ils] risquent de s'égarer dans trop de miroirs' (*2*, p.350). They manage to terrorise the white population, but with the only means at their disposal — *la parade* — and run the risk thereby, in revolutionary terms, of ending in 'le pur imaginaire' (*2*, pp.116-17). Their activity is therefore 'plus révolte poétique et jouée que volonté d'un changement radical' (*2*, pp.204-05). As Ville de Saint-Nazaire says to the blacks who have been conducting the ceremony, 'vous, vous n'étiez là que pour la parade' (*10*, p.110); the real action was elsewhere.

Or was it? In the character of Ville de Saint-Nazaire and the events which he reports, we come up against an aspect of the play which has very wide implications for an interpretation of Genet's concept of theatre, and for the extent to which Genet has any sort of political message to convey through a play such as *Les Nègres*. Is

Genet looking for a passage from the ritual that is such an important feature of his theatre to some kind of social reality which refuses ritualisation?

The first question that must be asked is the status of events that are merely reported on stage, as opposed to being shown. We are familiar with the device as it occurs in Greek and French classical theatre, and audiences have learned to accept the convention of the 'reality' of such events. But that was in a tradition where reality was seen as a continuum, a coherent whole, where what happened both on- and off-stage was governed by the same immutable laws as governed the lives of the audience/participants. Here, in *Les Nègres*, Genet is making a radical distinction between the sacred, the ritualisation of experience, which happens on stage, and the profane, the everyday world of non-theatre. Ville de Saint-Nazaire's dress, his language, his manner, all underline the fact that he represents a different world. And as in traditional society, the sacred is always the 'real', whereas the profane is in some way 'non-real'. In any case, these events are filtered through the stage, 'cette maison d'illusions' *par excellence*, as Dort calls it (*34*, p.131). What is the nature of the stage-character who is reporting these events? Whose words is he using?

Aside from these speculations of a general order, there are many indications that we are not to take the events off-stage as indicative of a serious political purpose. For instance, the only tangible sign of the execution of the traitor is the sound of the gun being fired, a sound that is on the frontier between the stage and off-stage, since it happens off-stage but is heard by the audience. But what do we hear? Not a pistol-shot, but a derisory 'bruit de pétard'. And what of the act for which the off-stage black is being executed? It is, in fact, treason. But treason for Genet is not judged according to normal codes of morality. For him it is one of the most desirable of crimes — because one of the most terrible. If one is determined to push to its limits the evil that one is accused of being, then treason is an appropriate means to that end. As the blacks' aim is to sever any remaining links with the white world, so Genet, through treason, will also break the bonds which tied him, not to enemies, but to friends.

The resulting isolation is wholly admirable to Genet: 'C'est peut-être leur solitude morale — à quoi j'aspire — qui me fait admirer les traîtres et les aimer. ...Car j'aurai brisé les liens les plus solides du monde: les liens de l'amour m'unissant au soldat volé' (7, pp.50-52). Elsewhere he speaks of 'la trahison abjecte. Celle que ne justifiera aucune héroïque excuse'. For it to be totally committed to evil, 'il suffit [...] que le traître ait conscience de sa trahison, qu'il la veuille et qu'il sache briser ces liens d'amour qui l'unissaient aux hommes' (7, p.276). This glorification of treason which is at the heart of Genet's world is clearly light-years from the prosaic, everyday crime committed by the off-stage black, which is judged in terms of normal social morality. It is difficult to see Genet taking it seriously in any sense that matters to him.

He has in fact made many statements on the relationship between literature and politics which are of direct or indirect relevance to Les Nègres. In the often-quoted Playboy interview, for example, he affects a lack of interest in whether Les Nègres serves the Negro cause, and suspects that in fact it doesn't (15, p.22). Indeed, it shouldn't: 'Plus une oeuvre est proche de la perfection, plus elle se renferme sur elle-même' (17, p.41). The world of the theatre is inherently 'safe', precisely because, being fantasy, it has no repercussions in the real world (16, p.28). Its very ineffectuality is its strength. He makes a revealing distinction between the concept of murder, which can be beautiful, and real murder, which is something quite different (16, p.30). Life and literature are not to be confused: when asked in this same interview why he had never committed a murder himself, Genet replied, 'Probablement parce que j'ai écrit mes livres' (16, p.31). As Archibald says, 'Un comédien... un Nègre... s'ils veulent tuer, irréalisent même leurs couteaux' (10, p.112).

Martin Esslin has written that the weak point of Le Balcon is the plot that Genet has to invent in order to hold the ritual together (37, p.217). Could one not argue the same for Les Nègres? Esslin does not, in fact: for him, the play succeeds through being ritual and nothing else, leaving on one side the question of the sub-plot in the wings. But there is a sense in which Genet has only invented this sub-plot in order to lend unreality to the ritual. Without the sub-plot the ceremony might begin to exist really, and Genet's whole tower of illusion would begin to collapse.

It is perhaps of interest to note here the ambiguity of black reaction to the highly-acclaimed 1961 production in New York of the English-language version of *Les Nègres*. Although the play made a significant impact on the development of black American theatre in the '60s — Leroi Jones's *Great Goodness of Life* is clearly influenced by *Les Nègres*, while reversing many of its themes — initial reaction was hostile, precisely because the play was judged too 'theatrical', the political message insufficiently clear: 'Genet fut accusé de rien connaître aux Noirs et à leur histoire: la pièce fut jugée sans rapport réel avec les conflits raciaux aux Etats Unis; la solution suggérée par Genet pour la libération des Noirs parut strictement théâtrale et sans liens avec la réalité américaine' (*38*, p.62).

It remains true that in the later years of his life Genet seemed to abandon creative writing and devote himself to political causes, notably the Black Panther movement and the Palestinian cause. It is tempting to look for some overall coherence in Genet's two-pronged revolt, and a certain coherence there obviously is. It is remarkable, for instance, how closely Genet's vision of the black world as portrayed in *Un Captif amoureux* reflects the original vision of *Les Nègres* thirty years previously, although it is in fact recalling his experience with the Panthers fifteen and more years after the writing of *Les Nègres*. For Genet, unlike for most writers, the imaginative experience came first, the 'real' one, faithfully reflecting it, later. As Moraly says, 'La vie de Genet est écrite. Tout (amours, aventures, désespoirs) obéit au rythme de l'écriture, seule importante' (*26*, p.17). But Genet constantly refers to this early imaginative experience — with no pejorative overtones — as 'rêve', or 'rêverie' (*18*, pp.6,10). Any ambiguity relates rather to the later political involvement which, as I have indicated, is often appreciated for its 'parade' rather than for its efficacy, and not to his literary production.

It would seem, therefore, that what interests Genet far more than any political concern is the opportunity in a play such as *Les Nègres* for pursuing the ontological quest which was the guiding obsession of his existence. Like Genet himself, the blacks are in pursuit of their being, but it is a pursuit which is doomed to failure, since the image they seek is merely the reflection of the fears and prejudices of a white world. As Dort points out, in a comparison between *Les Nègres* and *Les Bonnes*, 'Ni ses Bonnes ni ses Nègres ne sont véritablement des domestiques ou des Noirs: ils sont des bonnes telles que les rêvent et les craignent leurs patronnes, des nègres tels que, Blancs et tous plus ou moins racistes, nous les imaginons' (*34*, p.130). Because they can never coincide with their image, they have all sorts of difficulties with the roles they are playing: Neige is recalcitrant from the start, unwilling to commit herself in proper terms to the ceremony, and both Village and Diouf are reluctant and fearful to take it to its conclusion. They are all constantly being brought to heel by Archibald, since they have difficulty in maintaining the appropriate tone and language. The action on which the ceremony is based seems contradictory and full of holes: the victim is first found down on the waterfront, then 'derrière son comptoir' (though Neige insists Village had said she was 'assise à sa machine à coudre', *10*, p.60), then finally the café scene is forgotten in order to concentrate on the apparent relationship between the victim and her mother in bed upstairs. The members of the Court, on the other hand, have no such difficulties: fixed for ever behind their masks, they have only their parts to learn and repeat eternally every night. When Félicité accuses the Queen of being 'une ruine', she replies 'Mais quelle ruine! Et je n'ai pas fini de me sculpter, de me denteler, de me travailler en forme de ruine. Eternelle. Ce n'est pas le temps qui me corrode, ce n'est pas la fatigue qui me fait m'abandonner, c'est la mort qui me compose...' (*10*, p.103). What the Queen has achieved, the blacks are still pursuing. History, says Genet, is a witness to this need to bequeath to the future 'des images fabuleuses, agissantes à long, à très long terme, après la mort' (*2*, p.354): Christ, Saint-Just, the Black Panthers are all illustrations of this need. It is a reflection of the need for 'théâtralité', which remains the same from age to age, 'si elle est ce besoin de proposer non des signes mais des images complètes, compactes dissimulant une réalité qui est peut-être une absence d'être. Le vide' (*10*, p.355).

Because Genet's blacks are nothing, pursuit of the image is therefore all. And there must be no half-measures, no conciliation: the image must be as monstrous, as caricatured, as obscene as possible. This in itself is liberating: Robert Liensol, in the interview already quoted, speaks of the 'immense défoulement' that acting in Genet's play occasioned (*49*). Like Genet, the blacks are condemned to 'aller jusqu'au bout de la honte', but the acceptance of this negative vocation is a source of catharsis. Hence the exaggeration and violence of the image of *négritude* which the audience is offered. The bizarre, the grotesque and the frankly obscene mingle in Archibald's exhortation to the others:

> Que les Nègres se nègrent. Qu'ils s'obstinent jusqu'à la folie dans ce qu'on les condamne à être, dans leur ébène, dans leur odeur, dans l'oeil jaune, dans leurs goûts cannibales. Qu'ils ne se contentent pas de manger les Blancs, mais qu'ils se cuisent entre eux. Qu'ils inventent des recettes pour les tibias, les rotules, les jarrets, les lèvres épaisses, que sais-je, des sauces inconnues, des hoquets, des rots, des pets, qui gonfleront un jazz délétère, une peinture, une danse criminelles. Que si l'on change à notre égard, Nègres, ce ne soit par l'indulgence, mais la terreur! (*10*, p.60)

Village, in the fantastic tale of the White Woman, tells how 'on la prit un jour, on l'enferma et on la brûla', and Neige, 'riant aux éclats', adds, 'Ensuite on mangera les morceaux' (*10*, p.76). One is reminded, in its excess and in the violence of its challenge, of Césaire's *Cahier d'un retour au pays natal*, where we find for instance the following lines:

> Parce que nous vous haïssons vous et votre raison, nous nous réclamons de la démence précoce de la folie flamboyante du cannibalisme tenace. (*65*, p.73)

In the eyes of white authority, the black world forms an entity, so that not only the blacks themselves but the whole of their environment is seen as a threat. A grotesque parody of this vision is given in the descent of the Court to the African jungle, where

> Tout est marécages, fondrières, flèches, félins... ici les serpents pondent par la peau du ventre des oeufs d'où s'envolent des enfants aux yeux crevés ... les fourmis vous criblent de vinaigre ou de flèches ... les lianes s'amourachent de vous, vous baisent sur la bouche et vous mangent [...] tout est lèpres, sorcelleries, dangers, folies... (*10*, p.93)

Even the flowers are 'vénéneuses. Mortelles', and plants from the white world are 'assassinées par celles des tropiques' (*10*, p.94). Again, one recalls Césaire's

> nous chantons les fleurs vénéneuses éclatant dans des prairies furibondes... (*65*, p.83)

Césaire's surrealist cult of unreason in the service of *négritude* is parallel to the absolute opposition Genet establishes between the rational white world and willed black irrationality. One thinks also of Senghor's '*l'émotion est nègre, comme la raison hellène*'[7] although Genet follows the violence of Césaire or Soyinka (as the latter indicated by opposing *tigritude* to *négritude*, the tiger does not argue about its nature, it pounces and eats its prey), rather than the compromises of Senghor. 'Nous nous obstinerons dans la déraison, dans le refus' (*10*, p.41), says Archibald; since reason is a 'white' virtue, therefore identified with good, the blacks have no alternative but to cultivate its opposite in its most extreme form. It is a whole civilisation that is called into question; the Queen gives a kind of global parody of its elements in her confrontation with Félicité, thus

---

[7] Léopold Sédar Senghor, 'Ce que l'homme noir apporte' (first published 1939), in *Liberté 1: Négritude et humanisme*, Paris: Seuil, 1964, p.24. Senghor's italics.

effectively preventing the white audience from identifying with them as virtues:

> A moi, vierges du Parthénon, ange du portail de Reims, colonnes valériennes, Musset, Chopin, Vincent d'Indy, cuisine française, Soldat Inconnu, chansons tyroliennes, principes cartésiens, ordonnance de Le Nôtre, coquelicots, bleuets, un brin de coquetterie, jardins de curés... (*10*, pp.55-56)

The classical virtues are firmly white, and must therefore be rejected by blacks. Genet apparently saw this at work in the United States, during his stay with the Panthers. He quotes one of them as declaring 'A vos raisons, nous n'opposons d'abord des raisons contraires, mais des ricanements et des insultes' (*2*, p.298). There can be no common approach, no dialogue, because the white man has appropriated to himself the means of dialogue, reason itself.

From this it is quite clear which role Diouf is called upon to play in *Les Nègres*. He is the voice of 'raison, conciliation' (*10*, p.41), he wants to propose to the white world 'un accord, une entente' (*10*, p.42), but by doing so he accepts totally the terms of that world. Diouf is virtuous, but with white virtue: 'Sur ma tête comme sur la vôtre, légère et insupportable, est descendue se poser la bonté des Blancs. Sur mon épaule droite leur intelligence, sur la gauche tout un vol de vertus, et quelquefois, dans ma main, en l'ouvrant, je découvrais blottie leur charité' (*10*, p.44). In a passage such as this, one hears all the helpless rage of the young Genet, obliged to accept the charitable goodness of his benefactors, and to be grateful for it, while having nothing to offer in return. Sartre records an anecdote which Genet apparently told him: 'Une dame lui disait, "Ma bonne doit être heureuse, je lui donne mes robes." "Très bien," répondit-il, "Vous donne-t-elle les siennes?" ' (*28*, p.18). The sense of total dependence on another, so that one exists only as a projection of another's goodness and self-congratulation, is unbearable. But when the dependent creature turns round and bites the hand that feeds it, the result is incomprehension, stupefaction. As the Queen begins to realise the attitude of the blacks to her, she exclaims, weeping, 'Mais qu'est-ce que je leur ai fait? Je suis bonne, douce, et belle!' (*10*, p.108). The Missionary continues the protest: 'Montrez un peu de bonne volonté. Regardez comme elle s'est habillée pour vous rendre visite et songez à tout ce que nous avons fait pour vous. Nous vous avons baptisés! Tous! L'eau qu'il a fallu pour vous ondoyer? Et le sel? Le sel sur vos langues? Des tonnes de sel arraché durement des mines' (*10*, p.108).

Diouf also stands for harmony and equilibrium. Genet's humour in unmasking the nature and the impossibility of this equilibrium is scornful and final. In the episode of the Communion host (*10*, p.43), when the Missionary asks Diouf 'Inventerez-vous une hostie noire?...' Diouf replies 'Mais, Monseigneur, nous avons mille ingrédients: nous la teindrons', and suggests 'Une hostie grise'. When this is rejected by the Governor, Diouf comes back plaintively 'Blanche d'un côté, noire de l'autre?' Was Genet thinking specifically of Senghor in his portrayal of Diouf? The Senegalese leader was often criticised by the more militant strand of *négritude*, represented by Césaire, for his approach to the problems of black-white relations, based as it was on compromise and negotiation. One should note also the title of a volume of Senghor's poetry published in 1948: *Hosties noires*.

Anne Murch has an intriguing explanation of Diouf's role. She sees the whole play as an inversion of the normal structure of a religious rite, which from a basic asymmetry (priest and faithful) proceeds to the symmetry of a unified act of worship. Genet starts from asymmetry (stage and audience, black and white, masked and unmasked, etc.), but aggravates that asymmetry in the course of the ritual, by increasing the distance between the various participants. Diouf therefore, by proposing harmony and reconciliation, in other words, by attempting to restore to the rite its original purpose, is enemy no. 1 (*54*, p.252).

His position is, however, untenable. If one can talk of linear development in this play, then Diouf's status has clearly changed by the end. Firstly, he is the one designated to play the role of the white woman in the *simulacre*, in a double disguise — of colour and sex

— which only emphasises the derisory nature of his role. On his 'death', he ascends to the white heaven, from where he perceives a new vision of things, a new order:

> Des rapports nouveaux s'établissent avec les choses, et ces choses deviennent nécessaires. [...] C'est en effet une très curieuse nouveauté, la nécessité. L'harmonie me ravissait. J'avais quitté le règne de la gratuité où je vous voyais gesticuler. Même cette haine que nous leur portons et qui monte vers eux, je ne la distinguais plus. (*10*, p.91)

This sense of a harmonious whole from which the blacks are necessarily excluded is paralleled in a passage in the *Journal du voleur*, where Genet comments on the effect the 'normal', right-thinking world had on him as an adolescent:

> Exclu par ma naissance et par mes goûts d'un ordre social je n'en distinguais pas la diversité. J'en admirais la parfaite cohérence qui me refusait. J'étais stupéfait devant un édifice si rigoureux dont les détails se comprenaient contre moi. (*7*, p.205)

All he senses is his difference, the disharmony between himself and the rest of the world, lending a kind of monolithic coherence to that world.

Once Diouf has experienced the protective harmony of the white world, he is unable to leave it. He pleads: 'Je suis vieux... on pourrait m'oublier... et puis enfin ils m'ont enveloppé d'une si jolie robe...' (*10*, p.111). The black who had been playing the part of the Valet, now unmasked, replies: 'Garde-la. S'ils t'ont rendu pareil à l'image qu'ils veulent avoir de nous, reste avec eux. Tu nous encombrerais' (ibid.). He therefore joins the white world in death, to be numbered among those who have already realised their image, becoming 'l'Admirable Mère des Héros morts en croyant nous tuer, dévorés par nos fourmis et nos rages' (*10*, p.121). Like the brothel clients in *Le Balcon*, who aspire to *be* the figures they imitate — the Judge, the General, the Bishop, etc. — without having to perform the functions which in everyday life would have led to the dignity, he finally achieves the image in the white world to which he aspires.

Diouf has to disappear for wanting to reconcile the irreconcilable. A suggestion of the possibility of a real loving relationship between two individuals is made, however, in the characters of Village and Vertu. They are practically unique in Genet's literary output as an example of an apparently normal heterosexual relationship, at least in potential. There is a brief moment of tenderness between Irma and the Chief of Police in *Le Balcon*, but it is short-lived, and does not appear to lead anywhere. In *Les Nègres* the relationship is shot through with ambiguity and frustration, partly because of the way in which Genet intermingles it with the re-enactment of Village's pursuit and murder of the White Woman. The deeper ambiguity lies, however, in the fine balance between love and hate which they are obliged to adopt. As blacks, as 'nègres', love is forbidden them; Archibald tells Village, 'Tu es un Nègre et un comédien. Ni l'un ni l'autre ne connaîtront l'amour' (*10*, p.49). As in the 'sad clown' tradition, where the clown is seen as essentially unloved, so here love is only for the white world, and when Village insists that he wants Vertu for his wife, Archibald angrily tells him to go and join the (white) audience — 'S'ils vous acceptent ... Mais faites-vous d'abord décolorer' (ibid.).

Because of this, Village is obliged to express his love through hatred. In his evocation of how he first saw Vertu, he recalls how 'j'eus tout à coup, je crois, durant une seconde, la force de nier tout ce qui n'était pas vous...' But the moment did not last: 'Je ne pus supporter la condamnation du monde. Et je me suis mis à vous haïr quand tout en vous m'eût rendu insupportable le mépris des hommes, et ce mépris insupportable mon amour pour vous. Exactement, je vous hais' (*10*, pp.45-46). After a burlesque interruption from the Court, he continues, 'Je vous hais de remplir de douceur mes yeux noirs. Je vous hais de m'obliger à ce dur travail qui consiste à vous écarter de moi, à vous haïr...' (*10*, p.46). This extraordinarily convoluted emotional logic here speaks for itself. Its power lies in its ring of authenticity: as Genet claims in the *Playboy* interview, blacks talk like that. Hatred does not come naturally: Genet has always insisted on the self-sacrifice and suffering that is necessary in the pursuit of evil for evil's sake. If it were something easy or enjoyable, then it would be pursued as a good, and the 'normal' — here, white — world would have won.

The ambiguity of Village's relationship with Vertu is echoed in his attitude towards the white woman whose rape and murder are re-enacted, because the two are made at several points to overlap. Village is accused by the others of having loved the white woman, an accusation which he vigorously rejects, but nevertheless, when addressing Vertu at one moment he evokes 'la limpidité de votre oeil bleu, cette larme qui brille au coin, votre gorge de ciel' (*10*, p.72) and, conversely, turning to the Masque, he recalls 'vos pieds dont la plante a la couleur des pervenches, vos pieds vernis sur le dessus, ils se promenaient sur le ciment...' (*10*, p.73).

In spite of this confusion between their relationship and the ritual action, it is clear that the Village-Vertu love-theme is supposed in some way to be pointing 'off stage'. 'Attention, Village, n'allez pas évoquer notre vie hors d'ici', warns Archibald (*10*, p.45) — in itself a splendid piece of theatrical underlining to which I shall have occasion to return. In the final scene between the couple — which, perhaps significantly, closes the play in terms at least of its dialogue — we are confronted, for the first time, with apparently 'real' people, displaying 'real' emotions. The ceremony is over: for once they are 'noirs' and not 'nègres'. Genet indicates as much in the notes on 'Pour jouer *Les Nègres*' which precede the play: 'Il faudrait, aussi, que Village et Vertu quittent vers la fin, le rôle de convention qu'ils sont censés tenir pour cette fête, et dessinent les personnages plus humains de deux êtres qui s'aiment pour de bon' (*10*, pp.10-11). But the learned gestures of love are all white, the language of love is white, and they have to start from the beginning to find expression for their emotion. This would seem to hold out a ray of hope for some sort of future for the blacks which is not in one way or another conditioned by white models. It is probably the only moment in the play too where we feel that the characters are speaking in total sincerity, where words mean what they are supposed to mean. But the ending dissipates this impression. In the printed text, and so on stage, the black back-cloth is raised, to reveal all the blacks standing around the coffin, as at the beginning. The Minuet from Mozart's *Don Giovanni* starts up again, and Village and Vertu go towards the others, turning their backs on the audience. The ritual is about to repeat itself, and the implication is that it will always be so.

And so the ceremony is all. 'Nous sommes au théâtre', and any illusion we might have had that theatre points to something outside itself is precisely that, an illusion. It is perhaps the moment now to turn to a closer scrutiny of this ritual and the use Genet makes of it.

2. Ritual and Role

> 'Pretence! Reality! Go to hell, the
> whole lot of you!'
> (Pirandello, *Six Characters in Search
> of an Author*)

All of Genet's theatre depends to a greater or lesser extent on the transformation through ritual of everyday experience. His strong myth-making capacities, which provide the inspiration for the prison novels, are rendered tangible for the stage in a series of implicit or explicit rituals, from *Haute surveillance* onwards. This ritualisation is sometimes a substitute for action in a real world, when circumstances preclude the exercise of such action, sometimes the expression of a kind of transcendence, but always bears witness to the absolute rupture Genet posits between the world of the everyday and the world of the theatre. In all his pronouncements on the subject, Genet expresses his contempt for a theatre which is the mere repetition of the everyday. In the notes published under the title 'Comment jouer *Les Bonnes*' he claims: 'Sans pouvoir dire au juste ce qu'est le théâtre je sais ce que je lui refuse d'être: la description de gestes quotidiens vue de l'extérieur' (*3*, p.269). He even goes so far as to refuse to put on stage any phenomenon that cannot be transformed. A lighted match, for example, has no place in the theatre, because it is no different on stage from what it is in real life (*8*, p.47). There is a similarly revealing passage in the same series of letters to Roger Blin on the production of *Les Paravents*, where he criticises directors who look for models 'dans la vie visible et pas dans la vie poétique, c'est-à-dire celle qu'on découvre quelquefois vers les confins de la mort'. He continues: 'Là, les visages ne sont plus roses, les gestes ne permettent pas d'ouvrir une porte — ou alors c'est une drôle de porte et donnant sur quoi!' (*8*, p.16).

This is not to say, of course, that all theatre happens on stage: Genet's writings are full of instances of the ritualisation of everyday experience. Theft for example is frequently ritualised. 'Le cambriolage au moment qu'on le fait est toujours le dernier, ... cette unicité d'un acte qui se développe ... en gestes conscients, ... lui accorde encore ici la valeur d'un rite religieux' (*7*, p.33). The intense animation of the world as experienced by the thief at the moment of the theft recalls the frenzy of the African night as Village works up to his crime. Of the former, Genet writes: 'Ma peur portait le nom de panique. De chaque objet, elle en libérait l'esprit qui n'attendait que mon tremblement pour s'émouvoir. Autour de moi le monde inanimé frémissait doucement' (*7*, p.143).

In his criticism of what he sees as the bourgeois theatre with its literal approach and its psychological realism, Genet has, of course, many affinities with Artaud. It is uncertain how much Genet knew of Artaud when writing *Les Nègres*. Paule Thévenin, a friend and associate of both writers, asserted, in conversation with me, that Genet had read Artaud at that time, although Roger Blin insists that he was in fact very little influenced by him (*27b*, p.39). Similarities there are, however. Like Genet, Artaud revolted against the frivolity of what he terms a 'théâtre digestif' (*61*, p.121), producing only 'spectacles de distraction' (*62*, p.82), and the idea that the theatre should be concerned first and foremost with the psychological analysis of character. There are striking similarities in their general approach to the spirit of theatre: Artaud's evocation of the 'esprit d'anarchie profonde qui est à la base de toute poésie' (*58*, p.41) could equally well be Genet's, as could his declaration that 'le théâtre contemporain est en décadence parce qu'il a perdu le sentiment d'un côté du sérieux et de l'autre du rire' (*58*, p.40), a more surprising statement perhaps from Artaud, given that he is not usually associated with a pursuit of 'le rire'. That it is, however, a fundamental trait in his reflections on theatre is indicated in the words HUMOUR-DESTRUCTION, in large capitals, in the 'Premier Manifeste du théâtre de la cruauté', a formula which could be applied

as it stands to *Les Nègres*. Given the relationship Genet makes
between his theatre and a state of dream, which we saw in the last
chapter, an obvious parallel can also be drawn with Artaud's
identification of 'les images de la poésie' and dreams, especially
since he continues: 'Et le public croira aux rêves du théâtre à
condition qu'il les prenne vraiment pour des rêves et non pour un
calque de la réalité' (*62*, p.83).

There are similarities too in the interpretation of this general
spirit for the stage, sometimes springing from their common interest
in the oriental theatre. Artaud's passion for Balinese theatre is well-
known; Genet had less opportunity to pursue something which
obviously fired his imagination — he apparently had occasion to
witness oriental theatre only once, significantly perhaps in 1955,
when he saw a performance of Chinese theatre in Paris (*41*, p.64),
but the preface to *Les Bonnes* contrasts Japanese, Chinese and
Balinese theatre favourably with its Western counterpart. Both
Artaud and Genet are aiming at a kind of 'poésie dans l'espace'
(Artaud's term), by means of the transformation of the material of
theatre into signs, metaphors, symbols. Both find in the language of
gesture and attitude, and in the use of dance, music and so forth, a
vehicle for true dramatic performance, so that both objects and the
human body are 'élevés à la dignité de signes'. Genet, like Artaud,
was interested in the sound as much as in the articulation of
discursive language, and sought a mode '[qui] utilise des vibrations
et des qualités de voix' (*60*, p.88).

But although there is a similarity in general approach, and
sometimes in the means adopted, these means are frequently used by
Genet to a very different end from that aimed at by Artaud. Leaving
on one side for the present the whole question of their very different
approach to language, a consideration of Genet's use of ritual in *Les
Nègres* is revealing of notable dissimilarities.

Firstly, although the ritual re-enactment of the killing of the
White Woman forms the main action of the play, Genet is at pains to
present it as a parody. The essence of ritual is that the participants *all*
believe in its reality, all the time, while retaining that distance which
is the essence of theatre. As Genet himself says, 'Une représentation

... est vaine si je ne crois pas à ce que je vois qui cessera — qui n'aura jamais existé — quand le rideau tombera' (*11*, p.15). But the ceremony in *Les Nègres* turns out to be a reluctant one. The fact that all the blacks are playing roles with which they can never finally identify means that they stand outside them for a good deal of the time, constantly breaking down the audience's belief in what they are witnessing. As we have already noted, several of the characters are unwilling to go ahead with the ceremony at certain points. The ceremony is presented as dangerous, and the participants are fearful. 'Ne continue pas', says Vertu, 'affolée', as Village continues with his 'récit' (*10*, p.72). Archibald has difficulty in finding an actor willing to play the Masque, and Diouf is finally an unwilling recruit: 'Vous êtes sûrs qu'on ne pourrait pas se passer du simulacre?', he asks, 'geignard' (*10*, p.63). Genet constantly emphasises elsewhere the difficulty of the cult of evil. In the *Journal du voleur* he considers 'comme il est difficile d'accéder à la lumière en crevant l'abcès de honte' (*7*, p.75), and speaks of 'l'ascension ... difficile, douloureuse, qui conduit à l'humiliation' (*7*, p.102).

Abrupt changes in register are another way in which Genet undermines the solemnity of the ceremony, and this is something to which we will return in the next chapter. Sometimes this is done by using the complementary nature of the Court and the blacks acting the ritual, with burlesque comments by the former on the latter, or comments which are *hors de propos*. For example, the Valet and the Missionary exchange comments about their missing chairs as Village breaks in with his 'Notre couleur n'est pas une tache de vinasse qui déchire un visage, notre visage n'est pas un chacal qui dévore ceux qu'il regarde...', only to have the Governor cry out in alarm 'Vous les entendez? Il faut intervenir. Vite. La Reine doit parler. Madame, sautez du lit!' (*10*, p.53). At another point Village interrupts his own account of the murder, as he suddenly realises Diouf is not appropriately dressed: 'Ecoutez chanter mes cuisses! Ecoutez! (*Soudain il s'interrompt et désigne le masque qui tricote.*) Mais il n'a pas de jupon! Qu'est-ce que c'est que cette mascarade? J'arrête ma tirade si on ne lui fout pas une jupe' (*10*, p.67).

Throughout, there is the idea that the ritual is something fixed, that cannot be changed — but that this is somehow against nature. They are constantly having to be reminded that the ritual is special: 'Ici c'est le théâtre, non la ville', says Archibald, 'furieux', as they once more adopt an everyday tone (*10*, p.66). They get confused as to where they are in the text: when Village wants to carry on after a break, saying 'Je reprends plus haut... "La lune"...', Bobo interjects 'Pas du tout, c'est déjà récité' (*10*, p.67). The importance of the text is underlined by Archibald when he says 'C'est à moi qu'il faut obéir. Et au texte que nous avons mis au point' (*10*, p.31) and again, 'Vous n'avez pas le droit de rien changer au cérémonial' (ibid.). The Queen receives a curtly negative reply when she asks 'Ne pourrait-on pas précipiter le dénouement? Je suis lasse et leur odeur me suffoque' (*10*, p.56). Her role-playing stance is further emphasised by the stage-direction which follows immediately: '*Elle feint de s'évanouir*'.

The implied personal element in the second part of the Queen's remark just referred to is another element that has to be excluded from the ritual, and which they have difficulty doing. They must avoid the intimate 'tu' when addressing each other, preferring the more formal 'vous' (*10*, pp.44, 74). Personal emotions must be suppressed: Bobo criticises Neige's petulance, saying, 'Vous faites intervenir votre tempérament, vos colères, vos humeurs, vos indispositions, et vous n'en avez pas le droit' (*10*, p.29). Neither do the actors have the right to bring in their personal, 'non-theatre', lives: when Village begins to talk of the effect Vertu first had on him, Archibald calls him to order: 'Attention, Village, n'allez pas évoquer votre vie hors d'ici' (*10*, p.45). The fact, of course, that all these reflections are made by stage characters on the roles they are supposed to be playing emphasises the distance between themselves and their roles, and contributes to the overall effect of unreality. Ultimately, this is a source of comfort to them: before the white Court descends to revenge the White Woman's murder, Archibald calms Village's fears with the reassuring 'Ne crains rien, il s'agit d'une comédie' (*10*, p.89).

'Comédie' or not, the ritual has to be performed to the end. The distance established between actor and role only underlines the fact that this is not a 'normal' ritual, whose purpose is to unite all participants, but rather a ceremony of hatred destined to divide. If Genet's ceremonies resemble a Mass, it is a Black one, with Evil replacing Good as the transcendence which it reflects, a transcendence which Genet claims is at the heart of ritual (*16*, p.31). But having said that, it is necessary also to emphasise that this Evil is cultivated only because the Good which is the natural focus of human aspiration is forbidden. Paradise is lost, and can be an object only of nostalgia. Hence the difficulty in this cultivation of hatred. Neither the black nor the actor can know love: Village is constantly accused by the others of having loved his white victim, instead of using his sexuality merely as a means of power, and the ambiguities in the Village-Vertu relationship which we have already noted spring from this obligation to hate. Hatred and the cult of evil are not merely directed against the white world; if that were so it would be too easy. Anyone can hate the oppressor. But hatred here has to permeate every area of the lives of the blacks. To desire evil before all else means that love for the lovable is also rendered impossible. Just as Genet is obliged to betray his friends, so the blacks have to suppress all personal feeling in the ceremony of hatred to which they are condemned.

There is a suggestion that something else is possible, that an end to hatred could be envisaged, in the expressed conflict between the blacks involved in the ritual and Ville de Saint-Nazaire. When Archibald remarks that 'Il n'y a rien de nouveau, au moins, dans la cérémonie' (*10*, p.87), Ville de Saint-Nazaire bursts out angrily: 'Vous voulez donc continuer à l'infini? La perpétuer jusqu'à la mort de la race? Tant que la terre tournera autour du soleil ... dans une chambre secrète, des Nègres...' and Bobo breaks in 'Haïront! Oui, monsieur.' The conflict here is not merely between hatred and more positive relationships, but between two opposing conceptions of time. Ville de Saint-Nazaire, belonging as he does to the 'real' world of sequential events, sees time in linear fashion. Hatred governs time for a particular period, after which something else comes to take its place. The other blacks however are completely locked into ritual time, an unending series of cyclic movements destined to repeat themselves eternally, and no intrusion from the 'real' world is going to break the cycle. It is surely significant that the blacks pick up the ceremony again and continue it to the end, *after* the announcement by Ville de Saint-Nazaire of the execution of the traitor off-stage. From the ending, where the blacks are once again standing around the coffin as at the beginning of the play, we are led to believe that the ritual will commence again the following night and every night. Theatre is for Genet precisely the ritual repetition which denies historical time. As he says in 'L'étrange mot d'...': 'Entre autres, le théâtre aura pour but de nous faire échapper au temps, que l'on dit historique, mais qui est théologique. Dès le début de l'événement théâtral, le temps qui va s'écouler n'appartient à aucun calendrier répertorié' (*4*, p.10). The fact that *Les Nègres* is composed of only one act and unfolds therefore without a break, increases the sense of ritual and the inexorable process in which the actors are engaged.

There is even a suggestion that the cyclic process will continue 'beyond' the play, in some sort of future which is still not part of linear, historical time, but rather a manifestation of a larger cyclic movement, when the Queen, before her ritual slaughter, threatens to return 'dans dix mille ans...' (*10*, p.122).[8] The Queen is already in a sense 'outside time', fixed in an image from which there is no escape, but which is beyond mortality. The blacks on the other hand have all this still to create. Is it worth it? the Queen asks Félicité: 'Un long travail sur des continents et des siècles pour te sculpter finalement un sépulcre peut-être moins beau que le mien' (*10*, p.107).

In the sterility of the Queen's dead image can be seen figured the sterility of Genet's particular interpretation of 'l'éternel retour'. True ritual is after all based on a harmonious relationship with the outside world, the cyclic return of natural processes, inevitable but fruitful repetition. In *Les Nègres*, the ritualisation of time has its origin in the tension between an absolute rejection of the mirror

---

[8] Brustein suggests that we have here the final moment of the two cycles of civilisation, one represented by the ending of the play, the other by this threatened return of the Queen. He recalls Vico's images of the crowing of cocks and ominous thundering at the end of such cycles (*32*, p.409).

image (the white world) and the compulsive need to go on contemplating it.

The same undermining of the purpose of ritual can be seen in Genet's handling of the concept of the victim. Outwardly, this seems to conform to those norms which ethnology has taught us to expect: as befits a sacrificial victim, the White Woman here is innocent, a mere anonymous representative of the opposing group, in this case the white race. The whole race is symbolically destroyed in this one figure. As the Judge says of the murder, 'C'était tuer toute notre race et nous tuer jusqu'à la fin du monde' (*10*, p.99). The fact that the victim is also raped is, of course, of considerable symbolic importance. Magnified sexual potency is an essential part of the white world's image of the black. The threat to the white world must be not only present and immediate, but have its continuity assured in the future. From the black point of view it is important also that this sexuality should be a ritualised expression of power, rather than signifying any bond of love. The Queen subscribes to this idea as she proclaims: 'je meurs ... étouffée par mon désir d'un Grand Nègre qui me tue' (*10*, p.121).

The victim is killed in effigy, however, and this causes the first problem. It could be interpreted as a way of linking the present with the past, when a 'real' victim was killed, through a ritual repeated in an eternal present. But Roger Caillois, in his analysis of modern carnival, points out its total lack of religious value. In his opinion this is because as soon as the human victim is replaced by an effigy, the rite tends to lose its expiatory function, discarding at the same time its double symbolism, on the one hand of past defilements, on the other of a new world order.[9] But in the case of *Les Nègres* the 'death' of the effigy is not real. Diouf, disguised as the Masque, and Village, merely go into the wings for the murder scene, where they are reported to be sitting on a bench chatting to one another. The effigy, having no life to start with, cannot die.

The whites, however, need more than an effigy. They need a real victim who really dies and whose corpse lies in a real coffin, otherwise they are unable to proceed with their act of vengeance

---

[9] *L'Homme et le sacré*, Gallimard, 1950, p.157.

which would subdue the blacks and reduce the threat. The whites operate according to the rule of law, as opposed to the law of instinct obeyed by the blacks, and the rule of law demands a victim for punishment to be possible. When the whole ceremony is revealed to be a hoax, the Court is first annoyed and then alarmed:

> LE JUGE: ...Il n'y avait personne dans la caisse et dites-nous pourquoi?
>
> ARCHIBALD, *triste*: Hélas, monsieur le Juge, il n'y avait pas de caisse non plus.
>
> LE GOUVERNEUR: Pas de caisse? Pas de caisse non plus? Ils nous tuent sans nous tuer et nous enferment dans pas de caisse non plus!...
>
> LE JUGE, *aux Nègres*: A vous écouter, il n'y aurait pas de crime puisque pas de cadavre, et pas de coupable puisque pas de crime. Mais qu'on ne s'y trompe pas: un mort, deux morts, un bataillon, une levée en masse de morts on s'en remettra, s'il faut ça pour nous venger; mais pas de mort du tout, cela pourrait nous tuer. (*10*, pp.99-100)

Just as the blacks, as *nègres*, exist only through the image the white world has of them, so the whites are totally dependent for their existence on the mirror-image of the blacks. If there is no corpse, if the blacks' hatred is shown to be as insubstantial as everything else, then the white race as a distinct entity is in danger of disappearance. It could not survive the innocence of the blacks.

This episode is perhaps only the most striking example of the unreality which surrounds the death-theme in *Les Nègres*. Death and the theatre are in any case indissolubly linked in Genet's mind: in 'L'étrange mot d'...', he maintains that in a modern city the only place to construct a theatre is the cemetery: 'La mort serait à la fois plus proche et plus légère, le théâtre plus grave' (*4*, p.14). In *Les Nègres*, the coffin as symbol of death occupies a visually prominent place, literally central. But it is revealed not only to be empty, but not in fact to exist at all. Once again, a gulf appears between the tangible theatrical sign and what it would normally signify. One is reminded of the expectations built up by the visual impression of Saïd's suitcase in *Les Paravents*, supposed to contain gifts for his bride, and the sudden shattering of these expectations in the revelation that the suitcase is in fact empty. It is the same with Genet's treatment of death throughout *Les Nègres*. The 'massacre' of the white Court at the end is surrounded with unreality. For a start, it is hardly a massacre at all, being turned into a suicide by the whites in order to deprive the blacks of the satisfaction of killing them. And then the manner of their death is highly burlesque: there are the ritual speeches beforehand — we recognise the Governor's 'lines' that he was learning at the beginning of the play — as each in turn comes forward to meet his death, the comic effect being reinforced by this repetition. Archibald's 'A l'abattoir!', and 'Au suivant!' recall Ubu's 'Dans la trappe!' as he massacres the Nobles in Jarry's play, and appeals to the same sense of the ludicrous. The fact that the pistol shot that is supposed to kill each one of them is represented on stage by a child's toy pistol-caps, and the way the characters collapse on top of each other in order to 'die' only reinforce the sense of burlesque. The unreal nature of their death is also underlined by the way the Governor dies in the 'wrong' place, and has to get up and collapse again in the middle of the stage. All the 'dead' characters at one point lift their heads to listen to what is going on. Death here is clearly an empty ritual, mere 'play-acting'.

It is also surrounded with ambiguity in its various other manifestations in the play. There is a certain confusion as to how the White Woman met her death, the 'plot', as we have seen, being confused in various important details: how, for instance, did her husband manage to find her corpse in the house on his return, when this was supposed to have been brought back by Village for the ceremony? The answer is, of course, that the details do not matter, since the event never took place anyhow. In so far as the Masque is only the ritual re-presentation of this dead White Woman who did not in any case die, any reality attaching to the 'death' of the Masque is removed. The death by execution of the black traitor in the

episode off-stage is equally ambiguous and uncertain, for reasons
which I have already outlined. Genet plays with the idea of death, as
he plays with everything else. In this respect it is worth recalling
perhaps the Latin origins of the word 'illusion': *in ludere*, 'in play'.[10]
What is possible in the illusion of the stage is another matter in real
life. Genet affirms twice in the interview with Fichte that a real-life
impulse towards murder was channelled into poetry, although even
in real life his dream was for a murder without a victim (*16*, p.31).
'Tuer un homme est le symbole du mal', however, as he maintains in
Pompes funèbres, and the specific reason for this given in the
Journal du voleur brings *Les Nègres* into focus: he claims to be
'hanté par l'idée d'un meurtre qui, irrémédiablement, me retrancherait
de votre monde' (*7*, p.120). Murder remains, significantly, a goal that
is both exemplary and unattainable.

        The lack of reality that is illustrated in Genet's treatment of
death finds its most constant expression in *Les Nègres* in the role-
playing to which all the characters are condemned. Much has already
been said in passing on this subject, since it is so central to any study
of the play, but there remain certain observations to be made.

        As was said at the beginning of this chapter, Genet's desire,
like Artaud's, was to go beyond the psychological analysis of
character on stage. Artaud admitted that his methods did not allow
for such analysis —— but who said that this was the purpose of
theatre in any case (*58*, p.40)? In *Les Nègres* Genet develops this
idea even further, wanting above all to destroy the idea of the
personnage, a pre-existent entity embodied by the actor. The
resulting layers of reality throw us back from one reflection to
another, so that it is impossible sometimes to tell what level of role-
playing is going on. What seems at first innocent is found on further
reflection to be a minefield of ambiguity. Take for example the
straightforward-sounding question asked by Archibald regarding
Diouf who, as the Masque, has developed a taste for the white world
which he no longer wants to quit. Archibald asks: 'Mais il joue
encore ou il parle en son nom?' (*10*, p.112). Who is being referred to

---

10 J. Huizinga, *Homo ludens. Essai sur la fonction sociale du jeu*, Gallimard,
Coll. 'Essais', 1951, p.32.

by the personal pronoun? Even an audience used to the sophistication of modern theatre will tend to assume a greater reality in the 'il [qui] parle en son nom' than in the one '[qui] joue encore' — until it realises that the being referred to is also an actor 'qui joue encore'. The same illusion is created right at the beginning of the play, when Archibald introduces the actors, telling the audience what their occupations are 'in real life'. 'Quittée cette scène', he says, 'nous sommes mêlés à votre vie' (*10*, p.27) — but the real actor of which the character speaking is only a double, is doubtless part of the lives of the audience in quite a different way. The black actors on stage, therefore — who, off-stage, if Genet is to be believed, are already playing the role to which they are condemned by white society — are playing on-stage the role of blacks (already 'nègres' rather than 'noirs') who are ritualising their roles as *nègres*, in yet another dimension of reality — or lack of it. In more than one sense there is no one on stage who is not playing a role — although Dort argues that Ville de Saint-Nazaire is a genuine *noir*, totally himself without reference to a white world, whereas all the other characters are *nègres*, in the white shadow (*33*, p.138). In the same way there are no whites, except those portrayed by black actors. Indeed, the only genuinely white beings on stage, as Dort points out, are the dolls that are born from under Diouf's skirts, miniature likenesses of the Court — but these are even less alive than the rest of the characters, 'representative of a white race petrified into immobility by a fascination with its own myths' (*25*, p.189).

The power of these assumed roles is, however, considerable. There is a danger inherent in taking on the appearance of another, felt instinctively by Genet, the audience and the cast alike. Genet admits in the *Journal du voleur* that 'J'ai vécu dans la peur des métamorphoses' (*7*, p.39), and Innes records that so intense was the experience of role-playing in *Les Nègres* for the actresses playing the parts of Félicité and the Queen that they began to exchange insults in real life and to cast evil spells on one another (*40*, p.158). One of the terrifying features of this kind of transformation is clearly the ease and speed with which it can happen (one thinks of Gregor Samsa in Kafka's *Metamorphosis*): if identity is always doubtful, if

one exists only as a shadow of something else, then one form is as
good as another. The otherwise inexplicable metamorphosis of the
Missionary into a cow after his castration and just before he dies can
be explained only in these terms — especially as he just as abruptly
regains his upright stature of Missionary, and his (now falsetto)
voice, before collapsing on the heap of bodies centre-stage.

Another instantaneous transformation of personality is of
course effected by the use of masks, and in *Les Nègres* Genet has
recourse to this device in two different circumstances. The use of
masks, from having become almost unknown in the nineteenth
century realist theatre, has experienced something of a renewal in the
twentieth century, partly under the influence of Oriental theatre —
Artaud was immensely impressed by the expressive possibilities of
the Balinese dancing masks, while before him Gordon Craig
exploited not only the Oriental tradition but also the then unknown
masks from Central and West Africa — partly as a result of a
renewed vision of the human body.[11] The use of masks relates the
theatre much more closely to the visual than to the verbal world, and
has affinities therefore with dance and the plastic arts. It is resolutely
anti-realist and anti-psychological, and is therefore aiming very
much in the same general direction as Genet in *Les Nègres*. Genet's
use of masks for the Court, for example, both exploits all the
traditional possibilities of the medium, while adding new ones that
are specific to his purpose.

The play opens with the instant visual impact of the masked
figures of the Court, in opposition to the unmasked blacks at stage
level. The audience is immediately allowed therefore to pick up
certain visual signals without any need for verbal explanation, or
subsequent psychological unfolding of character. The spectator's
apprehension of these figures is based on certain presuppositions, a
reading of the signs indicating role: the way in which the spectator
views the masked figures is not 'innocent'. The ease with which the
figures are 'read' depends on a caricatural element, the enlarging of

---

[11] For a discussion of the whole question of masks and their use, both in
ritual and in the theatre East and West, see *Le Masque. Du rite au théâtre*,
Paris, Edns du CNRS, 1985.

certain features to convey fundamental traits which are instantly recognisable as an essential part of the role.

The effect here is grotesque, largely because these are not 'real' white figures, but the image which the blacks have of the white world. Genet has succeeded brilliantly through the use of masks in conveying a visual impression of this image, whereas the converse image, that of blacks as seen by whites, depends much more on language for its transmission. Because of the caricatural element, the sense of unreality which is at the centre of the image is powerfully conveyed.

Another feature of the mask which is exploited to full effect here is its extra-temporality. The mask is fixed for ever in an eternal present, 'au point d'articulation entre la vie et la mort ... son expression cristallise un état auquel est parvenu le dieu ou le personnage représenté'.[12] The characters that compose the Court here are precisely in that limbo between life and death, fixed in the image created by the Other and incapable therefore of evolution, but endlessly working over the same image. As the Queen says in the passage already quoted, 'Je n'ai pas fini de me sculpter, de me denteler, de me travailler en forme de ruine' (*10*, p.103).

But, given the role-playing propensities of all the characters in *Les Nègres*, the members of the Court do not stay in this fixed form. One of the potentials of the mask is that it allows plurality, it permits instant metamorphosis, and this Genet exploits to the full. When Ville de Saint-Nazaire announces the execution of the traitor, the members of the Court immediately take off their masks, indicating a shift in role, becoming actors again, but putting them on once more when it is time to complete the ceremony. In Genet's hands the mask becomes a device for changing the level of reality but, as ever, this transformation is ambiguous. Genet specifies that the mask is the image of a white face, but 'posé de telle façon qu'on voie une large bande noire autour, et même les cheveux crépus' (*10*, p.20). The eyes that look out through the mask are therefore the black ones that have created the white image in the first place — but it is also the case that these black eyes, 'yeux de nègre', are created by the white world

---

[12] Germaine Dieterlen, quot. *31*, pp.282, 279.

which is figured on the mask. There is no end therefore to the reflection of white and black, and Genet's use of the mask is yet another highly effective means of conveying fundamental ambiguity and insubstantiality. It is the same in his treatment of the masking of Diouf. This is a double travesty, in that it involves a change both of colour and of sex, but as it takes place on stage we are in no doubt as to what has happened, in one sense at least. But in another we are left with an even greater ambiguity, since Diouf's masking turns into what is apparently a permanent metamorphosis. After his ritual murder, he goes up to the white 'Heaven', still masked, but for his account of the white world as he now sees it, takes off his mask. He is, however, still 'une Blanche' — or rather, as he says, from his improved vantage-point, 'une Rose' (*10*, p.91). He is initially uncomfortable in his new role, and floats linguistically between his identity as a 'Rose' and his former blackness, fumbling for his personal pronouns: 'Je vous — pardon — je nous vois ainsi... Nous, c'est-à-dire vous, nous sommes toujours étouffant dans un air lourd' (*10*, pp.90-91). The double travesty is confirmed, however, as Diouf joins the 'collection' and becomes 'demain, et pour les cérémonies à venir ... l'Admirable Mère des Héros morts en croyant nous tuer', as Archibald says (*10*, p.121).

Genet's use of masks recalls in some ways, of course, that of Pirandello. It is of particular interest that in the play that, in terms of theme, most resembles *Les Nègres*, *Six Characters in Search of an Author*, which exploits the play-within-a-play situation, Pirandello masks the actors when they take on their roles. Pirandello, like Genet, was intensely interested in the multiplicity of character, and had Genet's sense that the theatre was in some ways more real than life: the stage is 'a place where you play at being serious', he claims (*64*, p.64). His characters also take on roles given them by a hostile or indifferent society, or by society's need for final definition of its prominent figures: one thinks of Pirandello's Henry IV, condemned to the eternal appearance of a German Emperor, which appearance is finally more 'real' than the real historical person. He is trapped, 'fixed ... in the mask from which he has been unable to free himself' (*63*, p.58). But Pirandello, extolling the superiority of theatre over life,

tends to concentrate on the fixity of the image. As the Father says, in
Six Characters in Search of an Author, whereas the reality of people
in everyday life changes from day to day, 'our reality doesn't
change... It can't change... It can never be in any way different from
what it is... Because it is already fixed... Just as it is... For ever!' (*64*,
p.57). Where there are successive incarnations, successive
appearances taken on by a character, the sense of a being behind the
appearance remains firm: 'Son relativisme ne remet pas en question
l'être, il révèle seulement ses possibilités de truquages qui se situent
dans l'espace de l'équation: vrai + faux = l'être' (*46*, p.111). Genet, on
the contrary, as we have seen, uses appearance precisely to underline
the absence of anything else, the intense ambiguity surrounding the
very concept of being.

Krysinski points out a further parallel between Pirandello and
Genet in the character of Archibald, who has essentially the same
role as Hinkfuss in *Tonight We Improvise*, that of master-of-
ceremonies. 'Mais en même temps Archibald représente non
seulement le théâtre et son mécanisme, mais aussi les Nègres, l'idée
que les Blancs font des Nègres. Hinkfuss représente seulement le
théâtre' (*46*, p.118). Archibald's dual role makes him indeed an
interesting figure, moving ambiguously between his two
'appearances'. He is the one who orchestrates the ceremony: Genet
himself uses this image in 'Pour jouer *Les Nègres*', when he
stipulates that at the start of Village's tirade 'J'entre et je m'apporte...',
'Archibald prendra les gestes d'un chef d'orchestre, donnant la parole
tantôt à l'un tantôt à l'autre' (*10*, p.9). He is the one who has overall
control of the performance, admonishing the actors when they fail to
get the 'tone' right, or when they bring up points which are not
relevant to the ceremony. He has the greatest consciousness of the
theatre as theatre, and seems to act as a mouthpiece for Genet in his
comments on the nature of theatre, as for example (to Village): 'Tu
es un Nègre et un comédien. ... Nous sommes sur cette scène
semblables à des coupables qui, en prison, joueraient à être des
coupables' (*10*, p.49). Here he brings together the two 'appearances',
the 'Nègre' and the 'comédien', in both of which he of course shares.

In this latter role it is also possible to see a parallel with
Artaud's *metteur en scène*, who seems at times to be a kind of
omnipotent demiurge, creating the theatrical event at the moment of
performance. In Artaud's theatre, the 'vieille dualité entre l'auteur et
le metteur en scène' will be replaced by 'une sorte de Créateur
unique, à qui incombera la responsabilité double du spectacle et de
l'action' (*60*, pp.90-91). It is true that Archibald works from a text
from which no departure is possible, but it is 'le texte que nous avons
mis au point' (*10*, p.31). Richard Coe sees in him also a parody of the
traditional Mister Interlocutor accompanying the Edwardian Nigger
Minstrel shows, and in a play in which all roles contain some
element of parody, it is certainly a parallel to be retained (*22*, p.284).

No character in this play in the end escapes the necessity to
play a multiplicity of roles, all of which undermines the very notion
of character. The ritual permits only role-playing, and role-playing
leads to futher ritualisation. The endless repetition of this process is
admirably caught in Genet's own formulation of the task of the
dramatist:

> Si [le drame] a, chez l'auteur, sa fulgurante origine, c'est
> à lui de capter cette foudre et d'organiser, à partir de
> l'illumination qui montre le vide, une architecture
> verbale — c'est-à-dire grammaticale et cérémoniale —
> indiquant sournoisement que de ce vide s'arrache une
> apparence qui montre le vide. (*4*, p.13)

3. 'Cette architecture de vide et de mots'

> 'Ma victoire est verbale et je la dois à
> la somptuosité des termes...'
> (Genet, *Journal du voleur*)

The ground of being would seem to be void, as far as Genet is concerned. Or rather, subtending appearance is not the being that one expects, but only void. The self is a void that can be given any shape, any reality, by appearance (22, p.229), or perhaps at best a colourless and odourless fluid that takes on the form of the successive vessels into which it is poured. That Genet himself is conscious of the reality of this process is illustrated in a revealing passage in *Un Captif amoureux*, where he looks back over his life, analysing the gulf between people's perception of him and his own understanding of himself. He describes himself as 'une feuille de papier blanche', which can be folded and unfolded at will to create ever new and varied forms, as a child will transform a sheet of paper into 'une cocotte, un bateau, un oiseau, une flèche en papier ou un avion' (2, pp.204-05). In this way, Genet took on 'l'apparence d'une montagne, d'un précipice, d'un crime ou d'un accident mortel', and he expresses his surprise when people took this appearance for reality, the 'simulacre' for 'l'acte lui-même'. His whole life was thus 'composée de gestes sans conséquence subtilement boursouflés en actes d'audace'. He continues: 'Or quand je compris cela, que ma vie s'inscrivait en creux, ce creux devint aussi terrible qu'un gouffre. Le travail qu'on nomme damasquinage consiste à creuser à l'acide une plaque d'acier de dessins en creux où doivent s'incruster des fils d'or. En moi les fils d'or manquaient'. In other words, Genet perceives himself to lack the essential, 'les fils d'or', the element that makes something what it is. It is in this light perhaps that one can interpret Genet's pursuit of evil, figured in *Les Nègres* by the cult of hatred: evil can be seen as a lack, 'not-good', which is why it would be a mistake to consider Genet's absolute evil as in fact absolute good turned on its head. Genet's metaphysical evil is a lack of being, a void at the centre where being should be.

In order that this void should become palpable for the stage, however, it must be given shape and expression, space must be used in such a way as to render it tangible — theatre being 'avant tout un espace à remplir', as Artaud said (*59*, p.103) — and the resources of language must render its transmission possible. For J.-M. Magnan, Genet has succeeded in translating for the stage the 'architecture de vide et de mots' (*10*, p.122) which is the very definition of *Les Nègres*: 'Le plateau de théâtre, à partir des *Nègres*', he claims, 'accuse sans trêve et sur tous les tons le réel de son absence' (*24*, p.171).

From what we know of the first production of *Les Nègres*, which began its run at the Théâtre de Lutèce on 28 October 1959, the highly-acclaimed decor, by André Acquart, succeeded precisely in conveying this 'absence', as well as the 'poésie dans l'espace' which seems to have been part of Genet's larger vision. The decor was composed of a framework of steel scaffoldings, erected to form a series of levels, the upper one being used by the members of the Court in their role as spectators. It is worth noting in passing that the vogue of the use of scaffolding in theatrical production dates from this time, and Acquart was clearly one of the first to use such a device. The scaffolding for *Les Nègres* was, however, covered in asbestos fibre, which had certain important effects.[13] For a start, by this device, Acquart transformed the crudeness of the bare metal, reminiscent of a building site, into something rich and sumptuous, with an elegance of texture which Genet must have thoroughly approved of. The ambiguity of appearance and reality is also fully

---

[13] I base my comments here on the photographic slides of the production taken by André Acquart himself. He very kindly gave me a private showing of these slides, and for this and his discussion of the production with me I am most grateful.

maintained: it both is and is not scaffolding. It is given an appearance, a 'parure', which is totally in keeping with the spirit of the play. The material itself, the asbestos fibre, was important in creating an iridescent surface which broke up and reflected the light, rendering the texture living, as opposed to the deadness of bare metal, and reinforcing Blin's desire 'que le décor soit vivant, qu'il bouge, qu'il respire' (27b, p.41). It seems to have been the mobility of the decor, its lack of fixed definition, which appealed most to Blin: 'C'était un décor à la fois rigide et souple. Vu de l'orchestre, il avait l'air d'une sculpture géante. En jouant sur les éclairages, il prenait diverses formes, des couleurs et des tonalités différentes. Il reflétait l'action de la pièce et y prenait part' (ibid.). Behind this whole structure was hung a black backcloth, image of the void itself, in its capacity to absorb light and convey a sense of nothingness. The white faces which are projected on to it at a certain point, figuring yet another level of spectator, only increase the sense of void, while rendering it tangible.

The decor and the spatial dimensions which it creates and exploits are only one aspect of the use of space in *Les Nègres*, an interpretation of Genet's particular requirements which are built into the text. Acquart's steel framework enables considerable use to be made of the vertical dimension, but Genet in any case specifies '[un palier] allant jusqu'aux cintres, et semblable plutôt à une galerie [qui] fait le tour de la scène', for the Court. It is clear that Genet wanted thereby a hierarchisation of space, with the superior power and authority of the white figures represented through their physically higher position on the stage. They form also an oppressive presence from which there is no escape: at several points in the play one of the blacks comments that they are being watched/listened to. No doubt there are here echoes of Genet's prison existence. Jeannette Savona makes an interesting parallel between this lofty observation-post and the Panoptikon recalled by Michel Foucault in his account of the French penal system, *Surveiller et punir*. The Panoptikon, invented by Bentham in the eighteenth century, is a totally enclosed area in which prisoners who are isolated from each other can be watched from a central observation tower, without ever knowing exactly when or how. The constant uncertainty thus engendered adds to the prisoners' sense of threat and isolation (*29*, pp.129, 115). This vertical dimension, together with the obvious fact of supervision in a prison system, is certainly exploited by Genet in a way that has the ring of psychological truth about it. It can be extended also on to a more general level, to become a spatial representation of power relationships, since *Les Nègres* is clearly also a play about power. When the members of the Court are watching the ritual, and are in a position of superior force, they are in the gallery: when they embark on their punitive mission which ends in their destruction, they descend to the same level as the blacks. Conversely, when Diouf becomes 'une Rose', through final identification with his role, he 'ascends' to the white heaven — in the gallery. The different strata of reality are confused in this respect as elsewhere, however, since Diouf in his guise of white Masque is characterised as 'Porte du Ciel' by Neige (*10*, p.65).

The physical distance of the white Court, which remains a distinct and separate entity during most of the play, serves several other purposes. Firstly, it fixes the attention of the audience, by making comments on the action, interpreting the action for the audience, thereby emphasising its separateness. It also provides another, contrasting centre of interest for the audience, a counterpoint which is at one and the same time illuminating and confusing. Again, it emphasises in concrete terms the black/white divide, while retaining a certain ambiguity due to the obvious negro features beneath the white masks. And it provides a 'reflection' of the white audience, whose attention is constantly switching between 'the blacks', who are the physical embodiment of their fears, and a grotesque representation of their own world in the Court.

The spatial isolation of one group or one individual from another, or distinguishing different 'worlds', illustrated in the physical location of the Court in the gallery, finds expression in a number of other ways. For example, for a considerable part of the play, Félicité is seated in a throne-like armchair half-way up the scaffolding structure, at some distance from the others and facing the Court, while remaining slightly below it. In her implied role as

Mother, Earth-Goddess, it is appropriate that she should not be identified totally with the group, although they on occasion gather together beneath her, distinguishing themselves from the white Court (e.g. p.92). For her two 'Dahomey' speeches, she rises, emphasising her authority, but sits down again afterwards. For the second of these, she and the Queen 'sont face à face' (p.102), in a highly theatrical black-white confrontation. In the ensuing dialogue between the two of them, 'les deux femmes avancent côte à côte, et presque amicalement, face au public, et jusqu'à l'avant-scène' (p.103). The other actors have previously been drawn to each side of the stage, the blacks to the left on a sign from Félicité, and the Court to the right on one from the Queen. This use of black-white opposing blocks is frequent: in the build-up to this scene, for instance, the members of the Court, in the 'forêt' and determined on revenge, stop dead in their tracks, and then go backwards towards the point of entry, opposite the blacks who have begun to pursue them (p.96). This block movement helps to ritualise the action, underlining the starkness of the confrontation.

Village and Vertu are another couple who frequently find themselves spatially isolated from the others. Sometimes there seems an attempt to appeal to or identify with the audience, as when they detach themselves from the others with their obsessive thoughts of hatred and murder, and approach the audience (10, p.50). The same happens during the massacre of the Court, when their physical detachment from the others is a sign of their need to talk to each other in more private and personal language (10, p.116). At the very end, however, after their lyrical love-dialogue, which has taken place in isolation from the others, they move back towards the group around the catafalque, suggesting to the audience that nothing has changed and the ceremony is about to start all over again. It is significant that although they have made approaches to the audience previously, at this point they turn their backs on it.

Sometimes the physical isolation of one of the actors is emphasised by a heightened emotional atmosphere. This is the case as the climax to the *simulacre* builds up, when the 'main gantée de blanc' (belonging to Diouf/the Masque) comes out from behind the

screen and takes hold of Village's shoulder. While the others sing
snatches of chant to the tune of the *Dies irae*, Village appears to be
pulled towards the screen behind which, visibly fearful, he
eventually disappears. Diouf's isolation during the scene where he
pleads for love and reconciliation is conveyed somewhat differently,
as the Court bursts out laughing, and the other blacks block their ears
(*10*, p.42).

There is thus a principle of discontinuity, of rupture, at work in
the play, which is perceptible at all levels, and is a reflection of the
ontological rupture within the being Genet himself. The various
aspects of the organisation of space which we have considered so far
are part of a wider organisation of stage space into different 'worlds'
radically distinct but interpenetrable by the characters who assume
first one role and then another. These worlds are often grouped in
opposing pairs, the most fundamental of which is perhaps the basic
opposition between the sacred world of the rite and the profane
world which contrasts with it. The profane world in *Les Nègres* has
pointers to it from the stage, but in a sense it does not exist on stage.
The clearest example of it is represented by the action in the wings,
which we have already discussed. The only character who belongs
entirely to this profane reality is Ville de Saint-Nazaire. For the
others this reality is a reference-point, they are somehow implicated
in it, but they belong more fully to the sacred world of the rite. Off-
stage reality intrudes, for example, in the form of the revolver which
Village produces when describing the events leading up to the
murder (*10*, p.36). But this is undermined by the fact that it is the
same revolver which refuses to go off during the mock massacre of
the Court (*10*, p.115). Apart from this, their participation in an off-
stage reality is revealed in their account of their off-stage
occupations (*10*, p.27), or Archibald's injunction to Village not to
refer to his life outside the theatre (*10*, p.45). The separation and
intermingling of the two worlds are perhaps seen most clearly at the
moment when Vertu, the prostitute, claims she is, because of her
profession, 'la seule à aller jusqu'au bout de la honte' (*10*, p.48).

Onstage is the world of ritualised crime. But it is noteworthy
that, in spite of the obvious fact that this crime is at the centre of all

the action that we witness on stage, we never actually see it. 'Tragédie grecque et pudique' (*10*, p.86), the most important action happens in secret. The Masque and Village disappear 'derrière le paravent', where the re-enactment of the murder takes place — or does not, as we later learn. Alfred Simon has some interesting observations to make on this phenomenon in the more general context of ritual action and its relationship with myth (*42*, pp.259-60). He bases his reflections on the Zuñi of New Mexico, whose ritual buildings have no opening on to the street. The ritual action happens on a terrace to which access is gained by a ladder, while another ladder leads down into an inside chamber. What happens on the terrace is seen by all the participants in the rite, but in fact the most important part of the ceremony, 'la partie sacrée de l'action', happens in the inner chamber, viewed only by the initiated. The same phenomenon can be observed, he says, in Melanesia, where the spectators to the rite see only puppets above a palissade, animated by ritual dancers whose dance constitutes the significant part of the rite. 'Ainsi l'essence du drame rituel réside non dans le spectacle vu par les spectateurs, mais dans l'action invisible, généralement la danse secrète des acteurs. En fait on ne peut séparer l'une de l'autre. L'action visible renvoie à l'invisible' (*42*, pp.260-61). In *Les Nègres*, Genet uses this spatial distinction between what can be seen by the profane audience (including, of course, the Court), and what must remain secret, and also the principle of the visible action referring back to the invisible. But, as we have already shown, he undermines the notion of the mystery of the sacred by immediately de-sacralising it: Diouf and Village are seen chatting in the wings, waiting for their next entry.

A kind of extension to the ritual world can be seen in the evocations of Africa, which appears as a mythological entity which is, however, clearly distinguished in spatial terms from the ritual action on stage. When the blacks are discussing the stench that would arise from a corpse if they tried to re-use the same one night after night, Bobo says: 'La puanteur vous effraie, maintenant? C'est elle qui monte de ma terre africaine' (*10*, p.33). It is 'une odeur de charogne', which contrasts strongly with the characteristics of the

white race, here identified in negative terms, 'blafarde et inodore ...
privée d'odeurs animales, privée des pestilences de nos marécages'
(ibid.). A splendid evocation of the black world is contained in
Félicité's second 'Dahomey' speech (*10*, p.80), when she invokes the
'messieurs de Tombouctou .... Tribus couvertes d'or et de boue.
Tribus de la Pluie et du Vent ..., Princes des Hauts-Empires, princes
des pieds nus et des étriers de bois', but also 'Nègres des docks, des
usines, des bastringues, Nègres de chez Renault, Nègres de Citroën'.
It is the black presentation of the world which, seen through the eyes
of the white Court, becomes immediately hostile and menacing.
When the members of the Court descend to avenge the murder, the
black world becomes tangible on stage, through the verbalisation of
their fears (*10*, p.93).

It is the same world that Diouf quits ('Grand Pays Noir, je te
dis adieu' [*10*, p.63]), as he prepares to 'faire [ses] premiers pas dans
un monde nouveau'. 'Moi, Samba Graham Diouf, né dans les
marécages de l'Oubangui Chari, tristement je vous dis adieu. ...
Qu'on m'ouvre la porte, j'entrerai, je descendrai dans la mort que
vous me préparez' (*10*, p.62), he says, indicating a further 'world' to
which he is to be initiated before ascending to the white 'heaven'.
The idea of a passage from one world to another is clearly important
here, and reveals a further spatial theme in the play, that of the
journey. When Diouf arrives in the white Heaven, still masked as the
White Woman, the Queen comments: 'Le voyage a dû être pénible,
ma pauvre petite. Enfin vous retrouvez votre véritable famille. D'ici,
d'en haut, vous les verrez mieux' (*10*, p.88), emphasising the ascent
to the world which is 'superior' in two different respects: it is
'Heaven', and it is white. By contrast, the Court descends to the black
world on its journey to avenge the White Woman's death. This is a
journey that has to be well-prepared: the Missionary tells the Valet
to prepare 'le manteau, les bottes, un kilo de cerises et le cheval de
Sa Majesté' (*10*, p.89). The Governor is asked 'Vous avez les
parapluies?', and the Valet has also 'les cachets de quinine', and 'la
gourde de rhum, et bien pleine!' In this way, not only the difficulty
of the journey, but also the hostility and impenetrability of the black
world are emphasised.

A further journey is evoked in terms which this time recall the world of fairy-tale, as well as being set well and truly in a fantasy-world before the account even begins. When Vertu, uneasy at the length of time Village is taking over the simulation of the murder, remarks 'Il ne revient pas', Bobo replies: 'Il n'a pas eu le temps. D'abord, c'est très loin'. 'Comment, très loin?' retorts Vertu, 'C'est derrière le paravent', leaving the audience in no doubt as to the make-believe nature of the whole affair. But Bobo continues her account of the journey: 'Bien sûr. Mais en même temps ils doivent aller ailleurs. Traverser la chambre, passer le jardin, prendre un sentier de noisetiers qui tourne à gauche, écarter les ronces, jeter du sel devant eux, chausser des bottes, entrer dans un bois...' (*10*, p.85). The references to well-known fairy-tales lift the account out of the everyday and into the timeless world of myth and ritual where truth and illusion are ultimately one, while the use of 'Mais en même temps' posits the everyday, matter-of-fact world that juxtaposes the fairy-tale one.

This use by Genet of a 'temps non historié', which has circularity as its characteristic, has already been commented on. Genet exploits also, however, circularity in space, of which one manifestation is the concept of the centre, most marked in the positioning of the coffin centre-stage. Because of this crucial location in stage-space, the fact that it is subsequently revealed to be empty erodes the reality not only of part of the imaginative world figured on stage, but of the whole of it. Where the centre is void, the structure itself cannot but be illusory.

Another use of the centre-theme, more positive this time, is in the figure of Félicité, especially in her 'Dahomey' speeches. She becomes the magnetic centre of the black world as she calls the Nègres to her from the four corners of the world and from every kind of experience, but also, in her implied image as Mother Earth, she is everywhere.

Sometimes Genet's exploitation of circularity involves movement in space. The ritual dance that opens the play is an example of this, but it introduces us not into the 'safe' circularity of traditional ritual practice, rather into a disturbing and outwardly incomprehensible rite. The combination of the black faces and the 'air de Mozart qu'ils sifflent et fredonnent', the evening dress and the yellow shoes, the flowers that they pluck from their buttonholes and throw on to the coffin, symbol of death — all this is heavy with a menace that cannot but fill the audience with apprehension. The fact that the blacks are ready to repeat the dance at the end combines spatial circularity with temporal, underlining the atmosphere of menace. The same feeling of menace is present when, a little later, they counteract the stench of the 'non-existent' corpse by encircling it, lighting cigarettes and blowing the smoke towards the coffin. They do this 'cérémonieusement', humming a chant beginning 'Je les aimais mes blancs moutons' (10, p.35), the nursery-rhyme mode emphasising the ritual act, but the juxtaposition of the cigarettes and the funeral rite disturbs the audience's expectations of what ceremony is about. Menacing too is the way in which Félicité moves around the stage before her main confrontation with the Queen: a note indicates that 'Félicité fait alors une ou deux fois le tour de la scène pour venir provoquer, en la regardant dans les yeux et en lui tournant le dos, la Reine' (10, p.102).

Other dance-episodes occur in the course of the play, all performed by one or other of the blacks, and all as part of the ritual. Village's dance in front of the coffin precedes the choice of Diouf as Masque (10, p.61), and all the blacks begin to dance as Village evokes the way in which he ensnared the White Woman and lured her to her bedroom (10, p.70). In a slightly different tone, Bobo greets Diouf as Masque with a 'danse obscène' (10, p.66). All these dances represent a highly organised use of space, and all represent an aspect of the ritual of hatred, either through menace or insult.

The same ritualised use of space is evident in the way in which Genet frequently suggests an action by a brief symbolic sketching of it, sufficient to convey to the audience what the gesture is supposed to represent, but so highly stylised that the audience is in no doubt that this is theatrical reality and not the everyday world. When the blacks make their farewells to Diouf, they walk slowly backwards, 'en agitant doucement un petit mouchoir que les hommes ont tiré de leurs poches et les femmes de leur sein' (10, p.62). A little later, during the build-up to the murder re-enactment, Bobo plays the role of 'voisine' to 'Madame Marie', but instead of leaving the stage at the end of this episode, 'elle imite les gestes de la sortie, mais elle restera en scène, près de la coulisse, le regard dirigé vers l'extérieur, fixée dans une attitude de départ' (10, p.69). Village and Vertu likewise at one point make as if to go towards the audience, but Archibald restrains them, saying 'Non, non, inutile. Puisque nous sommes sur la scène, où tout est relatif, il suffira que je m'en aille à reculons pour réussir l'illusion théâtrale de vous écarter de moi' (10, p.50). This is the use of space at its most theatrical: not only does the deliberate stylisation make it quite clear which world we are operating in, but theatre exposes itself, comments on itself in an excess of self-conscious lucidity.

Any consideration of the theatrical use of space must, of course, take into account the audience. This is true to an exceptional degree in Les Nègres, which is different from most plays in that Genet, as it were, wrote a 'part' for the audience. The theatrical truism that a play exists only in performance has even more substance with regard to Les Nègres, therefore, since without the audience there is no play at all. Genet's stipulation for the audience, which precedes the text, is well known. The play, he says, was written by a white man for a white audience. If by any chance the audience contains no white member, then some white person must be invited — a symbolic figure who would be clad in a 'costume de cérémonie' and have a projector turned on him throughout the performance. If no white person accepts this role, white masks must be distributed to the black audience as they enter the theatre. And if they refuse, then a dummy must be used.

Genet is therefore absolutely clear that this is a play for white people — or rather, perhaps, against white people. As Genet himself asserts, 'Cette pièce est écrite non pour les Noirs, mais contre les Blancs' (13, p.100), thus underlining the negative movement of revolt that is at its centre. Dort goes so far as to say that Genet gives the whites the creative role, since the entire play is a product of their fantasies (33, p.140). The audience is certainly involved in the play from the very beginning. We are accustomed in the modern theatre to a certain interaction between stage and audience — characters address the members of the audience, for instance, underlining the theatrical nature of the experience, and running counter to the realist tradition in which the audience is required to forget the distance between stage and front-of-house, accepting the illusion for a part of everyday reality. Genet certainly uses this interaction: one of the spectators is called on stage, for instance, to hold Diouf's knitting, producing an effect akin to Brecht's *Verfremdungseffekt* (alienation effect). But Genet goes beyond this, in defining the very nature of the audience. He assumes a collectivity of interest and identification, a homogeneity in the audience, which can no longer be the normal heterogeneous collection of individuals. But he defines it in this way only in order to make it a more precise target. The audience in *Les Nègres* is summoned to collaborate in its own destruction. Let it be noted in passing that Genet himself is in a curious position vis-à-vis the audience. He can have no identity with it, since he is, as he says, a 'white black'. The same curious relationship must exist between a black member of the audience and the performance on stage.

The audience is thus part of the play from the start. Archibald addresses its members, specifying that 'Ce soir nous jouerons pour vous' (*10*, p.26), and again 'Ce soir, nous ne songerons qu'à vous divertir' (*10*, p.27) — the double meaning of 'divertir' being surely significant here. But at the same time it is kept at a distance. Firstly, the aim of the blacks is to 'rendre la communication impossible', and there are many instances in the play when the audience is quite simply kept in the dark. Secondly, from the outset it is repelled by the ceremony of hate, which requires the audience to be abused and insulted. The resulting relationship is one of intense contradiction, on the one hand close identification, on the other total estrangement. Hatred too is a relationship, albeit a negative one.

The audience is not only the object of abuse by the blacks on stage: it has an even closer relationship with the Court, which forms a kind of mirror-image of the audience. In the Court, the audience contemplates a grotesque version of itself, a caricature corresponding to the image that the blacks have of them. Court and audience form a framework at either side of the blacks, and within this framework the ritual action happens. The result of this is that the receiver of the theatrical 'message' is doubled, with the blacks addressing now one 'audience', now the other, sometimes both together. The resulting ambiguity adds to the general subversion of reality which is Genet's concern throughout.

This doubling, spatially and in terms of meaning, is one aspect of a more general phenomenon, occurring repeatedly in Genet's *oeuvre*, that is, the use of the mirror as an image for reality endlessly repeating itself. In *Les Nègres*, all the antitheses used by Genet — black/white, audience/Court, love/hate, life/death, sacred/profane etc. — can be interpreted as mirrors, in the sense that each 'pair' is self-contained, each element of the pair dependent on the other for existence, and throwing back its own reflection on the other in a ceaseless process that carries on to infinity, creating a surface brilliance that is the very essence of theatricality. In his letters to Roger Blin, Genet notes this process; for him 'La scène serait ... un lieu où non les reflets s'épuisent, mais où des éclats s'entrechoquent' (*8*, p.49). Sometimes, as in the case of the audience and the Court, the image is a parodic, deformed reflection of itself, sometimes its opposite, as in the black/white contrast — one thinks of Félicité and the Queen confronting each other on the stage — but even in the latter case the image that is thrown back is one of the fears and fantasies of the other rather than a genuinely distinct 'other'.

This infinite repetition of the image is part of the ambiguity of the mirror: endless multiplication is an integral part of a closed system from which one can never escape. The mirror closes in the reflected object precisely because of this endless repetition of an image to which one is ultimately condemned. It seems that Genet experienced, though from the outside, the anguish that the dual nature of the mirror can provoke in an individual, in this case his friend Stilitano, an account of whose experience he gives in the *Journal du voleur*. They entered a fairground Hall of Mirrors, one of those labyrinths, part mirror, part transparent glass, '[où l'on] bute désespérément contre sa propre image ou contre un visiteur coupé de nous par une vitre' (*7*, p.302); and after a while Stilitano was the only one not to have found his way out again. 'Stilitano, et lui seul, était pris, *visiblement* égaré dans les couloirs de verre. Personne ne pouvait l'entendre mais à ses gestes, à sa bouche, on comprenait qu'il hurlait de colère. ... Stilitano était seul. Tout le monde s'en était tiré, sauf lui. Etrangement l'univers se voila. L'ombre qui soudain recouvrait toutes choses et les gens c'était l'ombre de ma solitude en face de ce désespoir...' (ibid.).

From this endless play of mirrors, there is no exit. The self meets only its own image, with which, however, it never manages fully to coincide. There is indeed a suggestion in *Les Nègres* that if ever such coincidence became possible, the self would simply disappear, the theatre being the catalysing element. What is left to the blacks? asks Archibald — and within the term 'blacks', as we have seen, can be included all those who, like Genet, suffer alienation from their true being. The answer is, the theatre, where the endless process of role-playing and reflection is ideally performed. 'Nous jouerons à nous y réfléchir et lentement nous nous verrons, grand narcisse noir, disparaître dans son eau' (*10*, p.48). The desire to pass through the looking-glass does not find fulfilment in Wonderland, but in self-abolition. Even here, however, 'nous nous verrons ... disparaître'; the self continues to watch the self as it disappears, reflection upon reflection. 'Le théâtre devient sa propre métaphore' (*47*, p.844), and any suggestion that it refers outwards to a more everyday reality is an illusion.

Whether the organisation of space in *Les Nègres* revolves around the notion of antithesis, as in Genet's use of mirrors, or the stage-audience dialectic, or whether he is pointing up the unreality of the whole theatrical enterprise, as in his revelation of the emptiness of the ritual through the emptiness of the coffin, it is the void that is being made concrete for the stage. And language, that other element in the total theatrical process, which we have not so far considered in detail, is called upon to play the same role. The same structures that are apparent and made visible in the spatial organisation — for example the sacred/profane dichotomy — reappear in fact in Genet's use of language.

The most noticeable feature of the language of *Les Nègres* is its fragmentation. There is a principle of rupture at work here which means that we pass constantly from one level to another, from one register to another, and move in and out of the various 'worlds' Genet puts on stage. The audience is thus disorientated as a matter of principle. For what is the purpose of language in this play? Genet states it quite clearly from the beginning, in terms that we have already had occasion to quote: the ceremony is designed to 'rendre la communication impossible'. Language is to be used therefore in such a way as to obscure. Roland Barthes describes this process of rupture in a passage on Sade which could be applied equally well to Genet. What he calls 'le plaisir du texte [chez Sade] vient évidemment de certaines ruptures (ou de certaines collisions): des codes antipathiques (le noble et le trivial, par exemple) entrent en contact; des néologismes pompeux et dérisoires sont créés; des messages pornographiques viennent se mouler dans des phrases si pures qu'on les prendrait pour des exemples de grammaire. Comme dit la théorie du texte: la langue est redistribuée. Or *cette redistribution se fait toujours par coupure*'.[14] In *Les Nègres*, this 'coupure' has a particularised subversive purpose, but the result is the same.

For instance, in order to destroy any link of understanding or affectivity between the blacks and their white audience, they are enjoined by Archibald to 'inventer sinon des mots, des phrases qui coupent au lieu de lier' (*10*, p.37). The word 'père' is thus forbidden as a designation of 'le mâle qui engrossa la négresse de qui je suis né' (ibid.), which periphrasis is preferred. Likewise, the blacks admit to being 'menteurs', since the names Archibald gave the audience are in fact false (*10*, p.28). References are frequently obscured: when Archibald is telling Ville de Saint-Nazaire to get on with the business in the wings, he says 'Allez, mais allez donc les prévenir. Dites-leur bien que nous avons commencé. Qu'ils fassent leur travail comme nous allons faire le nôtre' (*10*, p.29). But who are these 'ils' referred to? The members of the audience are not in a position to know, and the plot is insufficiently clear to make them want to know, so little or no suspense is involved.

---

14 Roland Barthes, *Le Plaisir du texte*, Paris: Edns du Seuil, Coll. 'Points', 1973, p.14.

The principle of rupture which is at the heart of the play is made manifest in a number of different ways. The antithetical structure of a great deal of the writing is one of the principal means of conveying this sense of rupture linguistically. The couple blacks/Court is responsible for a considerable amount of change in tone and register, of deliberate clash which undermines the seriousness of the ceremony, or the reality of what is going on elsewhere. Examples are numerous: the intimacy of Village's and Vertu's efforts to express their feelings for each other is counterpointed with the ludicrous massacre-scene of the whites by the blacks (*10*, pp. 116-18), for instance, while Village's tortured but lyrical analysis of his first sight of Vertu is interrupted by the Valet and the Governor quoting the current coffee-prices (*10*, p.46), they, like the price of gold and other stock-market commodities, encapsulating the image of white world effortlessly exploiting black. When Village and the Masque have disappeared behind the screen, and the other blacks are chanting solemn verses, the Judge and the Governor, who has a telescope, exchange ribald comments on the rape that is supposedly going on out of sight (*10*, p.83). In another example, the whole of Neige's anger and scorn at her suspicions over Village's feelings for the White Woman are concentrated on the shameful meeting of two worlds: 'Venu de loin, de l'Oubangui ou du Tanganaïka, un immense amour venait mourir ici, lécher des chevilles blanches' (*10*, p.58).

These reflections of different 'worlds' which clash and interact at every level form an important structural element in the play. They are of course another aspect of the mirror-theme, which is sometimes not only concretised in this way, but implicit in the language itself. Take, for example, the following passage: Archibald, presenting the blacks to the audience, says 'Nous nous embellissons pour vous plaire', and then, referring to the Court, 'S'ils n'ont que leur nostalgie, qu'ils s'en enchantent' to which Neige replies, 'Le chagrin, Monsieur, leur est encore une parure'. The Queen a little later picks this up, asking 'Est-il vrai, Mademoiselle, qu'il ne nous reste que notre tristesse et qu'elle nous soit une parure?' and Archibald replies: 'Et nous n'avons pas fini de vous embellir. Ce soir encore nous sommes venus travailler à votre chagrin' (*10*, pp. 24-25). Language here is a series of reflections, slightly distorted each time, but refusing to lend meaning other than that conveyed by the surface brilliance. On other occasions the mirror-image is conveyed in language by a sense of infinite recession: the Queen, in her confrontation with Félicité, wonders why the latter should want to go on endlessly killing her. 'Mon sublime cadavre ... ne te suffit pas? Il te faut le cadavre du cadavre?' And Félicité replies: 'J'aurai le cadavre du fantôme de ton cadavre' (*10*, p.103).

The insubstantiality of personality creates another manifestation of rupture. Since the characters *are* nothing, they assume different linguistic patterns very readily. For the purposes of the ceremony, all the blacks take on one or more roles, and pass from one to the other with disturbing ease. Village turns from his ambiguously lyrical evocation of the White Woman, to the 'voix du récit', to the voice of the Masque, interposing these from time to time with his 'own' voice as actor. Vertu at one point takes on the voice of the Queen, claiming *comme somnambulique*: 'Je suis la Reine Occidentale à la pâleur de lis!' The Queen herself, still somnolent, joins in until she suddenly realises what is happening and wakens with a start: 'Assez! Et faites-les taire, ils ont volé ma voix! Au secours...' (*10*, p.55).

Sometimes rupture occurs within the same sequence, by language being given a deliberate twist to reveal and destroy its articulations. This is what seems to happen in the following exchange, where the tone begins as one of mock solemnity:

> LE JUGE: La Reine est endormie. ... Elle couve. Quoi? Les verrières de Chartres et les vestiges celtiques.
>
> LE GOUVERNEUR: Qu'on la réveille, nom de Dieu... le coup de la gamelle comme à la caserne...
>
> LE JUGE: Vous êtes fou? Et qui va couver? Vous?
>
> LE GOUVERNEUR, *penaud*: Je n'ai jamais su.

> LE VALET: Pas moi non plus. Surtout debout. [a
> reference to his missing chair] (*10*, p.52)

The mystery, albeit fake, of the Queen's dreams is completely destroyed.

If there is poetry here, it is of a negative kind, breaking down language by its refusal of normal communication. It is a poetry of hatred: 'Inventez non l'amour, mais la haine', says Archibald, 'et faites donc de la poésie, puisque c'est le seul domaine qu'il nous soit permis d'exploiter' (*10*, pp.37-38). The apparent illogicality of the 'donc' here is surely significant: for the blacks the poetry of hatred is the only one there is, and hatred in their situation necessarily gives rise to poetry. It is a poetry of outrage, of insolence, where every gesture is shot through with a defiance which demands the juxtaposition of nobility and vulgarity. Village, in his frenzied tirade in which the whole of black history is mingled with the love for Vertu which he is unable to express, declares: 'Je ne chantais pas, je ne dansais pas. Debout, royal, pour tout dire, une main sur la hanche, insolent, je pissais' (*10*, p.54). And again, evoking his insolently seductive entry into the White Woman's house: 'J'entre. Et je pète' (*10*, p.66).

In order to achieve their image, it is necessary for them to go 'jusqu'au bout de la honte' (*10*, p.48), and the violence of the language and imagery used in pursuit of this goal corresponds to the violence of that image. Sometimes the linguistic violence is such that it becomes clear that it corresponds to nothing in the real world, as for example in the 'cannibalism' passage already quoted, where the element of parody is considerable.

Parody clearly plays an important part in the construction of the image both of the blacks and the whites. The violence directed by the one against the other is often presented thus, causing it simply to evaporate in humour. Sometimes this is done by means of a simple play on words, as when Archibald declares to the Judge: 'Vous aurez la tête tranchée, mais tranchée en tranches' (*10*, p.117). Or the use of hyperbole renders solemnity ridiculous, as in the Governor's speech before his death: 'Je vais donc mourir, mais ce sera dans une apothéose, enlevé par dix mille adolescents plus maigres que la Peste et la Lèpre, exalté par la Rage et la Colère. ... Je meurs sans enfants... Mais je compte sur votre sens de l'honneur pour remettre mon uniforme taché de sang au musée de l'Armée' (*10*, p.115).

The use of hyperbole, and excess in language in general, is another aspect of the basic aim to make communication impossible. The blacks are going to hide in language by rendering it opaque: 'C'est par l'élongation que nous déformerons assez le langage pour nous en envelopper et nous y cacher: les maîtres procédant par contraction' (*10*, p.38) — the 'maîtres' being the writers of classicism in its various forms. In a striking image, Archibald says to Bobo: 'Vous vous régalez l'oreille de ces volubilis qui s'entortillent autour des piliers du monde' (*10*, p.38), where the climbing plant with its profusion of leaves and flowers is compared to language which embellishes and hides at one and the same time.

The necessity to hide their real thoughts and feelings is emphasised again when Archibald points out that they are being watched: 'Ne dites que ce qu'il faut dire, on nous épie' (*10*, p.40). In the context of this desire for secrecy, it is perhaps worth recalling Genet's reflections in *Un Captif amoureux*, firstly on a television transmission of a speech by the Black Panther Bobby Seale, at the time in prison awaiting execution. Genet did not at first understand the apparently anodyne speech, where Seale recalled his mother's cooking and his conjugal life. He then realised that what he said was in a kind of code, 'compris "supérieurement" ', and he recalls the way in which the Negro slaves on the plantations used to communicate with each other in a language which remained impenetrable to their white masters. 'La ruse de Bobby était du même ordre que les ruses des esclaves de plantations: sur des musiques africaines qui deviendront le jazz, ils faisaient passer des mots d'ordre de fuites et de révoltes' (*2*, p.269).

The exploitation of excess in language is also evident in Genet's use of lists, of which there are many. The poetry here is full of a kind of enraged energy, as in Neige's evocation of the 'Nègre' — 'balafré, puant, lippu, camus, mangeur, bouffeur, bâfreur de Blancs et de toutes les couleurs, bavant, suant, rotant, crachant, baiseur de boucs, toussant, pétant, lécheur de pieds blancs, feignant, malade, dégoulinant d'huile et de sueur, flasque et soumis' (*10*, p.36). Or it evaporates in its own excess: compare the Governor's list of tortures: 'Balle dans la tête et dans les jarrets, jets de salive, couteaux andalous, baïonnettes, revolver à bouchon, poisons de nos Médicis ..., crevaison de l'abdomen, abandon dans les neiges éternelles de nos glaciers indomptés, escopette corse, poing américain, guillotine, lacets, souliers, gale, épilepsie...' and so on (*10*, p.100).

The negative is apparent too in the 'insultes' directed against the white world in the form of the Masque, which form part of the ceremony, but here Genet exploits liturgical practice, specifying for example that the 'Litanie des Blêmes' be recited 'comme on récite à l'Eglise les litanies de la Vierge, d'une voix monocorde' (*10*, p.65). The musical parody here in Genet's use of liturgical plainchant, as in his exploitation of the 'Dies irae' and of the Mozart minuet, is an ironic application of 'white' cultural norms to a black situation. Neige continues in her turn, in an evocative passage where whiteness is seen to be the result of a kind of sickness: 'Moi aussi, je vous salue, Tour d'Ivoire, Porte du Ciel, ouverte à deux battants pour qu'entre, majestueux et puant, le Nègre. Mais que vous êtes blême! Quel mal vous ravage? Jouerez-vous ce soir la Dame aux camélias? Merveille que le mal qui vous fait toujours plus blanche et vous conduit à la blancheur définitive' (*10*, p.65). But she immediately undercuts the impact of this by pointing to the 'pauvre Nègre' hiding under the disguise of the white Masque.

The most positive use made of language is perhaps in the celebration of *négritude* itself, usually in the words of Félicité. Her 'Dahomey' speeches are ritualised expressions of blackness which do not, however, descend into cliché, and which avoid the negativity of evocations of the 'Nègre' seen through the eyes of the white world. Félicité's invocations have meaning, it is true, only by contrast with those of the white world, but it is a contrast which, like that implicit in the work of the poets of *négritude*, makes blackness into a value. Perhaps in spite of himself, Genet's tone is here affirmative.

The same affirmative tone, though perhaps on a more universal plane, is found in the language of the love-scenes between Village and Vertu. Their relationship stands outside the ceremony, and is criticised by the others precisely for this, and their language when evoking or addressing one another has a deeply personal character not found in the language of the ritual. Although their status as blacks is their starting-point, they are not addressing the audience, and these episodes are therefore less conditioned by the black-white confrontation than any other. They are nevertheless inextricably bound up with the ceremony, as Village's confusion between the characteristics of the White Woman and those of Vertu on several occasions makes clear, an indication of the ambiguity of their status within this ritual of hatred. Apart from these exchanges, the only point in the play when a genuine lyricism is attained is in the short incantatory poems which accompany the — unseen — climax to the simulacrum. Their liturgical role is emphasised by Genet's instruction that they should be sung to the chant of the *Dies irae*, and that the actors should 'y mettre beaucoup de grâce' (*10*, p.10). They are related to the action in so far as they revolve around the notion of silence and secrecy, while Neige evokes the theme of sacrifice and death in her 'Expire, expire doucement / Notre-Dame des Pélicans, / Jolie mouette, poliment, / Galamment, laisse-toi torturer' (*10*, p.82). The lyricism of these poems is clearly undercut by the supposed violence of the hidden act which is going on simultaneously.

In spite of these lyrical episodes, however, it is the corrosive potential of language which remains uppermost in the play. One of the principal aims of the blacks is after all to 'corroder, de dissoudre l'idée qu'ils voudraient que nous ayons d'eux' (*10*, p.110), that is, of the white world. Since poetry is all that is allowed them, they will exploit it to the full. In his interview with Michèle Manceaux on the Black Panthers, Genet identifies with their hatred of the white world and their desire to destroy it. Unable to do this alone, however, 'je ne pouvais que le pervertir, le corrompre un peu, ... ce que j'ai tenté de faire par une corruption du langage, c'est-à-dire à l'intérieur de cette langue française qui a l'air d'être si noble, qui l'est peut-être d'ailleurs, on ne sait jamais' (*17*, p.38). It is the most radical gesture that can be made, no doubt, when one does not possess in any real sense the means of expression. French is the language of France, and France is rejected by Genet in so far as France rejected him. The situation for Genet is akin to that of the colonised black. As Sartre says, 'comme les mots sont des idées, quand le nègre déclare en français qu'il rejette la culture française, il prend d'une main ce qu'il repousse de l'autre, il installe en lui, comme une broyeuse, l'appareil-à-penser de l'ennemi' (*67*, p.244). 'Une broyeuse', because the enemy's language, as Maurice Lecuyer points out, perpetuates the black's supposed inferiority, 'par suite des connotations péjoratives des termes se référant au noir' (*27c*, p.46). If he refuses this language, he finds himself 'devant un vide linguistique nécessairement signe d'un vide spirituel' (ibid.). For Genet, as a poet, there is only one solution to this dilemma. In his preface to George Jackson's *Soledad Brothers*, he writes '[The black man] has then only one recourse: to accept this language but to corrupt it so skilfully that the white men are caught in his trap.To accept it in all its richness, to increase that richness still further, and to suffuse it with all his obsessions and all his hatred of the white man' (*6*, p.22).

Such is the programme of *Les Nègres*, and Genet goes some distance here towards explaining the particularly striking but illusive features of his use of language in this play. To pervert the signs of civilisation itself, to cause a great gulf to appear between signifier and signified, so that normal meaning is destroyed and relationships are void — such is the most subversive and revolutionary programme possible, the perversion of perception and thought itself.

4. Conclusion

'Si dans l'oeuvre d'art le "bien" doit
apparaître, c'est par la grâce des
pouvoirs du chant, dont la vigueur, à
elle seule, saura magnifier le mal
exposé.'
(Genet, *Avertissement* to *Le Balcon*)

In *Les Nègres*, as in all Genet's writing, the corrosive power of
language is uppermost. It cannot be otherwise, given his
fundamental aim to subvert and destroy the system which he felt had
rejected him, while remaining chained to that system through his
compulsive need to express this rejection at every moment. Genet's
use of language is frequently obsessive: in the interview with Fichte,
he admits the fascination the French language has for him,
attributing this to the fact that French was the language he was
sentenced in (*16*, p.32). Just as the colonised is obliged to indict the
coloniser in the language of his oppressor, so Genet is condemned to
utter his 'long cri de révolte d'un homme seul' (*52*, p.37) in French,
while at the same time corrupting the vehicle to which he is
condemned. He seems to see this as the one active gesture he can
make in a world in which his role is essentially passive, where
reaction rather than action defines the frontiers of the everyday.

There is, however, a more positive role accorded to language
— or rather, it is possible to read this obsession in another and more
positive light. Language is, firstly, a refuge from an unbearable
reality. As Diouf says of Village, 'Si sa souffrance est trop forte, qu'il
se repose dans la parole' (*10*, p.47). It is also, on a more general
level, an attempt to rehabilitate experience, to give value to that
which has been rejected and reviled by society at large. Genet

attributes an almost magical power to the capacity of language to transform experience: language literally re-creates the objects it expresses. In the *Journal du voleur*, he writes of his early experience, saying:

> De cette période je parle avec émotion et je la magnifie, mais si des mots prestigieux, chargés, veux-je dire, à mon esprit de prestige plus que de sens, se proposent à moi, cela signifie peut-être que la misère qu'ils expriment et qui fut la mienne est elle aussi source de merveille. Je veux réhabiliter cette époque en l'écrivant avec les noms des choses les plus nobles. (*7*, p.65)

As Village says, 'L'esclavage m'a enseigné la danse et le chant' (*10*, p.54). The radical difference between art and life which we have constantly noted in the course of this study is again apparent here, and helps to explain why it is so important to underline the physical splendour and magnificence of staging in any production of Genet's plays. In one of his letters to Roger Blin, Genet applies this transmutation of the base matter of experience specifically to the theatre: 'L'Homme, la Femme, l'attitude ou la parole qui, dans la vie, apparaissent comme abjects, au théâtre doivent émerveiller, toujours, étonner, toujours, par leur élégance et leur force d'évidence' (*8*, p.37).

It is in passages such as this that one can again discern a strong similarity with Artaud, in his rejection of theatre as a copy of life, and his identification of theatre with *la Fête*. But Genet here also points away from Artaud, to an aspect of theatre in which his aims are ultimately quite different from those of Artaud, and that is in his belief in language, and particularly the written text. The principal meaning of the definition 'clownerie', which Genet gives to his play, is after all, according to *Robert*, 'pitrerie verbale'. For Artaud, articulated discourse should have no more significance in the theatre than it does in dreams (*60*, p.91): for Genet it is the principal means of recuperating the unacceptable and of destroying the enemy with his own weapons. His early prison experience is clearly of significance here: deprived of the means of action, the re-creation of experience through language was the only way open to him. Genet's use of language, however, often approaches Artaud's. Because rational, discursive language, the language of logic and dialogue belongs to the enemy, he celebrates the poetic, the anti-rationalist, the incantatory functions of language. This is particularly evident in *Les Nègres*, as we have seen, where these functions are used to obscure meaning and create a gulf between signifier and signified, and between emitter and receiver of the theatrical message.

It is one thing to say that language rehabilitates and gives value to that which was deprived of it. Genet, however, goes further, professing a total aestheticism by claiming that the act which gave rise to the art can be judged only through that art. In *Journal du voleur* in particular he insists on the validity of this approach. 'De la beauté de son expression dépend la beauté d'un acte moral' (7, p.24), he claims. The judgement of conventional moralists has no validity: 'S'ils peuvent me prouver qu'un acte est détestable par le mal qu'il fait, moi seul puis décider, par le chant qu'il soulève en moi, de sa beauté, de son élégance' (7, p.218). Transformation is essential: beauty must be accorded to that which has none, in order that the *chant* may be born: 'Le but de ce récit, c'est d'embellir mes aventures révolues, c'est-à-dire d'obtenir d'elles la beauté, découvrir en elles ce qui aujourd'hui suscitera le chant, seule preuve de cette beauté' (7, p.320). Genet is not, of course, the first to use this particular alchemy: one thinks of Baudelaire in his essay on Théophile Gautier: 'C'est un des privilèges prodigieux de l'Art que l'horrible, artistement exprimé, devienne beauté.'[15] So in *Les Nègres*, what was reviled will become beautiful, black will become a positive value instead of a negative. As Félicité says to the Queen, 'Pour vous, le noir était la couleur des curés, des croque-morts et des orphelins. Mais tout change. Ce qui est doux, bon, aimable et tendre sera noir. Le lait sera

---

[15] Baudelaire, 'Théophile Gautier' (I), in *Œuvres complètes*, vol. II, ed. C. Pichois, Gallimard, Bibl. de la Pléiade, 1976, p.123. Cf. also Simone Weil: 'Autant le malheur est hideux, autant l'expression vraie du malheur est souverainement belle' ('La personne et le sacré', in *Ecrits de Londres*, Gallimard, 1957, p.37).

noir, le sucre, le riz, le ciel, les colombes, l'espérance, seront noirs —
l'opéra aussi, où nous irons, noirs dans des Rolls noires, saluer des
rois noirs, entendre une musique de cuivre sous des lustres de cristal
noir...' (*10*, p.105). It is significant, however, that Félicité here
retains the white value-system, merely making it black, unlike the
perception of Village and Vertu at the end of the play, when they
realise that all will have to be created anew, and a new value-system
evolved.

Is there not in any case something of the Humpty Dumpty
about this transformation process, this resolute valorisation through
art which has art alone as its criterion? We have seen how Genet
firmly rejects the intervention of the real world in the literary
artefact. '[Le langage] ne change rien au monde, le met en
représentation de miroir en miroir' (*30*, p.407): language can only
reflect itself and what it represents, eternally, through the literary
process. If it is impotent in the real world, it is also safe: at the end
of *Les Nègres*, Village wonders how they are going to get rid of the
Court, since, 'sauf les fleurs, nous n'avons rien prévu: ni couteaux, ni
fusils, ni gibets, ni fleuves, ni baïonnettes. Pour nous débarrasser de
vous faudra-t-il qu'on vous égorge?' (*10*, p.113). The Queen replies:
'Pas la peine. Nous sommes des comédiens, notre massacre sera
lyrique.' In the same way, the Missionary's castration at the end is
purely verbal, since throughout the whole episode the blacks remain
'immobiles' (*10*, p.118). Genet suggests at one point that there is
power in this verbal victory, but, however it is defined, it remains on
a lyrical level: ' "Le pouvoir est au bout du fusil", peut-être, mais il
est quelquefois au bout de l'ombre ou de l'image du fusil' (*2*, p.117).

Such refusal to engage in the real world poses problems for
anyone who would try to assess Genet's work in moral terms. What
is then to be said in moral terms of the philosophy of hatred which
permeates *Les Nègres*? John Cruickshank believes that we are
obliged to judge Genet on the formal linguistic structures he
proposes to his readers, in other words as poetry which 'is almost
Mallarmean in its aesthetic purity' (*44*, p.205). He suggests that there
is an insoluble contradiction at the heart of Genet's work: if we
identify with Genet's outcasts, we will be led to ideas of social

reform, which Genet rejects. If we ignore the content of his works, we remain isolated from the only world of experience he cares to write about. But if we admire only the artistic presentation of this world, we accept literature as a phenomenon without moral existence. This is the highest form of nihilism, encompassing both the content of art and its formulation. This would certainly seem to be the way Genet often wants us to see his artistic endeavour. There is a sense in which this moral nihilism is essential to Genet's vision as it is translated in all his writings. Freedom is essential to moral action, and Genet's characters are never free. In *Les Nègres*, we have seen the way in which they are obliged to take on certain roles, how the endless interplay of mirror-images sends one reflection back to the other, how the capacity for a moral being to take his destiny in his own hands and make deliberate choices is so diminished as to become a law of the physical world — the choice of the mirror, part of the mineral world, as image for this process is surely significant. In such a world moral action becomes not only redundant, but impossible: the ontological sterility which is the fate of all Genet's characters is equalled by their moral sterility.

And yet, on the other hand, if we stand outside Genet's own view of things, it is possible to see Genet as mesmerised by the Good which he rejects, and therefore posing problems which have a substantial moral content. The quest for absolute Evil is nevertheless a quest for an absolute. It remains a nihilism, but one which can have profound moral implications. As Coe says, the essence of Genet's ambiguity lies in the fact that 'his moral nihilism crystallises for the reader the very substance of ethics ... with a clarity, a forcefulness and an urgency which no more positive attitude could hope to achieve' (*22*, p.310). Genet himself, at least in his later years, would not seem to be averse to the idea that his writing has a moral content. In the interview with Layla Shahid Barrada and Rüdiger Wischenbart, in 1983, Wischenbart suggested that 'Il y a presque un Jean Genet moraliste qui se découvre, qui apparaît', to which Genet replied: 'Ça ne me gêne pas que vous disiez ça de moi. Mais ne confondez pas moraliste avec moralisateur' (*18*, p.12). As Simone Weil said, the aspiration towards goodness is a fundamental human trait: 'Ceux qui choisissent le mal ou le prennent pour le bien, ou à quelque moment ont désespéré du bien'.[16] Genet would seem unquestionably to belong to the latter category.

We should not forget either that the whole of Genet's existence was devoted to a peculiar kind of *sainteté*, which he describes as 'le plus beau mot de la langue française' (7, p.243). Sainthood is seen as the resolution of a division within the self, as he illustrates in the *Journal du voleur*:

> Dieu: mon tribunal intime.
> La sainteté: l'union avec Dieu.
> Elle sera quand va cesser ce tribunal, c'est-à-dire que le juge et le jugé seront confondus.
> Un tribunal départage le bien et le mal. Il prononce une sentence, il inflige une peine.
> Je cesserai d'être le juge et l'accusé.[17]

Do not Genet's blacks reflect this same division, and the same impossible pursuit, through a perverse aestheticism, of a wholeness that eludes them? The choice of blacks to figure his particular predicament was remarkably apt, giving wider human and, dare one say it, historical dimensions to a situation which at base was deeply personal. That these historical dimensions are severely limited in scope and potential by Genet himself only adds to the play's universality. Black consciousness, especially in Africa, has moved on from the dialectic of *négritude* to a development of black values which owe little or nothing to a reaction against their white counterparts. Although the black *prise de conscience* at the time of decolonisation incarnated in a particularly effective way Genet's personal double-bind situation, it was the dramatic potential of the theme which was undoubtedly responsible for the great impact the

---

[16] Simone Weil, *Ecrits de Londres*, Gallimard, 1957, p.172.
[17] 7, p.279. Cf. Baudelaire's consciousness of this double role in e.g. 'L'Héautontimorouménos' (*Les Fleurs du Mal*): 'Je suis la plaie et le couteau! Je suis le soufflet et la joue! Je suis les membres et la roue! Et la victime et le bourreau!'

play has continued to have on the development of theatre, particularly in the United States, as a result of the immensely successful New York production by Gene Frankel, which opened in May 1961, although we have already noted the ambiguity of black reaction to this production. Not only did it act as a catalyst for the development of a black theatre in the United States, but it had an undoubted influence on such seminal figures as Grotowski and the phenomenon of the Living Theatre. Individual plays may well also owe something to this production. As well as Leroi Jones's *Great Goodness of Life*, already mentioned, Douglas Turner Ward's *Day of Absence*, 'A Satirical Fantasy', first performed in 1965 by the Negro Ensemble Company, uses an all black cast disguised as whites.[18]

A notion which may be helpful in the elucidation of Genet's peculiar moral and aesthetic standpoint is that of the baroque. However difficult it is to pin down to a clear aesthetic programme, the baroque seems to reflect many of the features of Genet's theatre. The play of antithesis, especially that of being and not-being, and the consequent question-mark over the very notion of being, is a fundamental part of the baroque aesthetic. There is the same endless and fruitless pursuit of a self which eludes the pursuer: 'Nous courons derrière un être qui nous fuit. ... Nous ne sommes jamais nous-mêmes, mais toujours en deça ou au-delà'.[19] Being can be sought only through representation, hence the importance in baroque theatre of disguise, masks, costume etc. As in Genet's theatre, the impossibility of grasping the essence of being is compensated for by an endless play on appearance, directly or indirectly translated by the phenomenon of the mirror, but a mirror which deforms rather than reflecting reality with strict accuracy. Indeed, the fundamental question of the baroque, which is taken up with equivalent intensity by Genet, is precisely: what is reality? It is true that in the baroque there is generally a total identification of theatre and life: all the

---

[18] I am indebted to Professor Gerald Rabkin of the Theatre Department, New Jersey, Rutgers University, for drawing this play to my attention, and for his useful comments on the impact of Gene Frankel's production.

[19] Claude-Gilbert Dubois, *Le Baroque: profondeurs de l'apparence*, Paris: Larousse, 1973, p.140.

world's a stage. But what Genet refused on stage was the ordinariness of life: in fact, the stage spilled over into life insofar as for Genet life took on meaning only when dramatised. Hence his highly individual and ambiguous approach to political reality.

Taking into account the complexities of *Les Nègres*, and the play's obvious power to disturb and provoke, can one talk in terms of success or failure? As an attempt to look outwards from the world of the theatre and make meaningful statements about the real world, the play must surely be categorised as a failure. The blacks remain ultimately imprisoned in the 'jeu des glaces' on stage, condemned to the spectacular world of appearance. 'Se voulant apothéose des apparences, il reste pris dans la glace des cérémonies', says Alfred Simon of Genet's theatre in general (*42*, p.257). But in some respects this is the way Genet wants it. He can see no role for a theatre which goes beyond itself, which is not totally self-sufficient. If *Les Nègres* is a failure, it is a willed one, and in any case a very splendid one. It is a question of willing what one has: just as the blacks are left only theatre as their field of action, only poetry as their means of expression, so Genet accepts what he is condemned to: 'Ecrire c'est peut-être ce qui reste quand on est chassé du domaine de la parole donnée' (*14*, n.p.).

Selective Bibliography

Note: Works in French are published in Paris unless otherwise stated.

A I - GENET: WORKS

(Genet's *Œuvres complètes* are published in 5 volumes by Gallimard, 1952-79. Items of particular interest to the present volume are given below, against the abbreviation *OC*, along with other items not collected there.)

1. *Le Balcon*, in *OC*, IV, Gallimard, 1968, pp.33-135.
2. *Un Captif amoureux*, Gallimard, 1986, 504p.
3. 'Comment jouer *Les Bonnes*', in *OC*, IV, Gallimard, 1968, pp.267-70.
4. 'L'étrange mot d'...', in *OC*, IV, Gallimard, 1968, pp.9-18.
5. *Haute surveillance*, in *OC*, IV, Gallimard, 1968, pp.9-18.
6. Introduction to George Jackson, *Soledad Brothers: The Prison Letters of George Jackson*, trans. Richard Howard, New York, Coward-McCann, 1970, n.p., Cape, London, 1971, pp.17-24.
7. *Journal du voleur*, Gallimard: Coll. Folio, 1982, 306p.
8. 'Lettres à Roger Blin', in *OC*, IV, Gallimard, 1968, pp.215-63.
9. *Les Nègres*, Décines (Isère): L'Arbalète, 1958.
10. *Les Nègres*, Gallimard: Coll. Folio, 1980, 123p.
11. 'Préface' to *Les Bonnes*, Edns J.-J. Pauvert, 1954, pp.11-17.
12. *Querelle de Brest*, in *OC*, III, Gallimard, 1953, pp.201-415.
13. *'L'art est le refuge...'* in Genet *et al.*, *Les Nègres au port de la lune: Genet et les différences*, La Différence, 1988, pp.99-102.

A II - GENET: INTERVIEWS

14. [Autoportrait], Vidéo-cassette, Coll. Témoins, 1982.
15. Interview, *Playboy*, IX, (Apr. 1964), 45-54; French version in *Magazine littéraire*, no. 174 (June 1981), 18-22.
16. Interview with Hubert Fichte, French version in *Magazine littéraire*, no.174 (June 1981), 23-37.

17. 'Jean Genet chez les Panthères noires' (Interview with Michèle
     Manceaux), *Le Nouvel Observateur* (25 May 1970), 38-41.
18. 'Une rencontre avec Jean Genet' (Interview with Rüdiger Wischenbart
     and Layla Shahid Barrada), *Revue d'études palestiniennes*, 21 (Aut.
     1986), 3-25.

B I - CRITICISM: BOOKS

a) Bibliography

19. Coe, Richard N., *Jean Genet: a checklist of his works in French,
     English and German, Australian Journal of French Studies*, VI (1969),
     113-30.
20. Webb, Richard C. and Suzanne A., *Jean Genet and his Critics: An
     Annotated Bibliography, 1943-80*, Metuchen, N.J. and London: The
     Scarecrow Press, 1982 (Scarecrow Author Bibliographies, no.58).

b) Books entirely devoted to Genet

21. Coe, Richard N. (ed.), *The Theatre of Jean Genet: A Casebook*, New
     York: Grove Press, 1970, 250p.
22. ——, *The Vision of Jean Genet*, London: Peter Owen, 1968, 343p.
     Also New York: Grove Press, 1969.
23. Dichy, Albert & Pascal Fouché, *Jean Genet, essai de chronologie,
     1910-1944*, Bibliothèque de littérature française contemporaine de
     l'Université de Paris VII, 1988.
24. Magnan, J.-M., *Jean Genet*, Seghers, Coll. Poètes d'aujourd'hui, 1966,
     191p.
25. McMahon, Joseph H., *The Imagination of Jean Genet*, New Haven:
     Yale University Press, and Paris: P.U.F., 1963, 272p.
26. Moraly, Jean-Bernard, *Jean Genet, la vie écrite: biographie*, La
     Différence, 1988.
27. *Obliques*, 2 (1972), numéro spécial Jean Genet. Includes
     a) Gitenet, Jean, 'Réalité profane et réalité sacrée dans le théâtre de
        Jean Genet', pp.70-73.
     b) Knapp, Bettina, 'Entretien avec Roger Blin', pp.39-43.
     c) Lecuyer, Maurice, '*Les Nègres* et au-delà', pp.44-47.
28. Sartre, Jean-Paul, *Saint Genet, comédien et martyr*, appeared as Vol. I
     of Jean Genet, *Œuvres complètes*, Gallimard, 1952, 579p.
29. Savona, Jeannette L., *Jean Genet*, Macmillan Modern Dramatists,
     London: Macmillan, 1983.

c) Theatre in general, including books with a chapter devoted to Genet

30. Abirached, Robert, *La Crise du personnage dans le théâtre moderne*, Grasset, 1978, 512p.

31. Aslan, Odette, 'Du rite au jeu masqué', in *Le Masque: du rite au théâtre*, Edns du CNRS, 1985, pp.279-89.

32. Brustein, Robert, *The Theatre of Revolt: An Approach to the Modern Drama*, Boston, Toronto: Little, Brown & Co., 1962.

33. Dort, Bernard, 'Le Jeu de Genet', in *Théâtre public*, Edns du Seuil, 1967, pp.136-44.

34. ———, 'Genet ou le combat avec le théâtre', in *Théâtres: essais*, Edns du Seuil, Coll. Points, 1986, pp.122-39.

35. ———, 'Pirandello et le théâtre français', in *Théâtre public*, Edns du Seuil, 1967.

36. Elam, Keir, *The Semiotics of Theatre and Drama*, London: Methuen, 1980.

37. Esslin, Martin, *The Theatre of the Absurd*, revised and enlarged edn, Harmondsworth: Penguin Books, 1968.

38. Fabre, Geneviève, *Le Théâtre noir aux Etats-Unis*, Edns du CNRS, 1982.

39. Fletcher, John, ed., *Forces in Modern French Drama. Studies in the permitted lie* (see especially Coe, Richard N., 'Genet', pp.147-67), Univ. of London Press, 1972.

40. Innes, Christopher, *Holy Theatre: Ritual and the avant-garde*, Cambridge U.P., 1981.

41. Pronko, Leonard C., 'Jean Genet', in *Theatre East and West: Perspectives towards a total theatre*, Univ. of California Press, 1967, pp.63-67.

42. Simon, Alfred, *Les Signes et les songes. Essai sur le théâtre et la fête*, Edns du Seuil, Coll. Esprit, 1976, 283p.

43. Ubersfeld, Anne, *Lire le théâtre*, Classiques du Peuple 'Critique', Edns Sociales, 1978, 304p.

B II - CRITICISM: ARTICLES

a) on Genet in general

44. Cruickshank, John, 'Jean Genet: The aesthetics of crime', *Critical Quarterly*, VI, 3 (Aut. 1964), 202-10.

45. Hoffmann-Liponska, Aleksandra, 'La conception du théâtre de Jean Genet et sa confrontation avec les thèses d'Antonin Artaud', *Studia Romanica Posnaniensia*, II (1972-73), pp.39-53.

46. Krysinski, Wladimir, 'Un rapprochement: Pirandello et Genet',
    Filoloski Pregled, III-IV (1968), pp.105-19.
47. Simon, Alfred, 'La métaphore primordiale', *Esprit*, XXX, 338 (May
    1965), pp.837-44.
48. Wilcocks, R.W.F., 'The theatre as ritual', in *21*, pp.201-10.

b) on *Les Nègres*

49. Craipeau, Maria, 'En répétition: *Les Nègres* de Jean Genet', *France-
    Observateur* (22 Oct. 1959).
50. Goldmann, Lucien, 'Micro-structures dans les vingt-cinq premières
    répliques des *Nègres* de Jean Genet', *Revue de l'institut de sociologie*,
    Université Libre de Bruxelles, 3 (1969), pp.363-80.
51. Graham-White, Anthony, 'Jean Genet and the psychology of
    colonialism', *Comparative Drama*, IV (1970), pp.208-16.
52. Kanters, Robert, [Jean Genet], *L'Express* (5 Nov. 1959).
53. Martin, Graham Dunstan, 'Racism in Genet's *Les Nègres*', *Modern
    Language Review*, LXX, 3 (July 1975), pp.518-25.
54. Murch, Anne, 'Je mime donc je suis — *Les Nègres* de Jean Genet',
    Revue des Sciences Humaines, XXXVIII, 150 (Apr.-June 1973), 249-
    59.
55. Piemme, Michel, 'Les Espaces scéniques et dramatiques dans *Les
    Nègres* de Jean Genet', *Marche Romane* (Univ. de Liège), XX (1970),
    39-52.
56. Sarraute, Claude, [Jean Genet], *Le Monde* (30 Oct. 1959).
57. Taubes, Susan, 'The white mask falls', *Tulane Drama Review,* Special
    Issue Ionesco and Genet, VII, 3 (Spring 1963), 85-92.

C I - OTHER WRITINGS: ON THEATRE

58. Artaud, Antonin, 'La Mise en scène et la métaphysique', *OC*, Vol. IV,
    Gallimard, 1978, pp.32-45.
59. ——, 'Première lettre sur le langage', *OC*, Vol. IV, Gallimard, 1978,
    pp.101-05.
60. ——, 'Le Théâtre de la cruauté: premier manifeste', *OC*, Vol. IV,
    Gallimard, 1978, pp.86-96.
61. ——, 'Le Théâtre de la cruauté: second manifeste', *OC*, Vol. IV,
    Gallimard, 1978, pp.118-24.
62. ——, 'Le Théâtre et la cruauté', *OC*, Vol. IV, Gallimard, 1978, pp.82-
    85.
63. Pirandello, Luigi, *Henry IV*, tr. Frederick May, Harmondsworth:
    Penguin Books, 1962.

64. ——, *Six Characters in Search of an Author*, tr. Frederick May, London: Heinemann, 1980.

C II - OTHER WRITINGS: GENERAL

65. Césaire, Aimé, *Cahier d'un retour au pays natal*, Edns Présence Africaine, 1971 (first published Bordas, 1947).
66. Memmi, Albert, *Portrait du colonisé*, Edns Jean-Jacques Pauvert, Coll. Libertés, 1966.
67. Sartre, J.-P., 'Orphée noir' (Introd. to L.S. Senghor, *Anthologie de la nouvelle poésie nègre et malgache*, Presses Universitaires de France, 1948), in *Situations*, III, Gallimard, 1949, pp.229-86.

CRITICAL GUIDES TO FRENCH TEXTS

edited by
Roger Little, Wolfgang van Emden, David Williams